A little piece of England in the sun

by

Bob Thompson

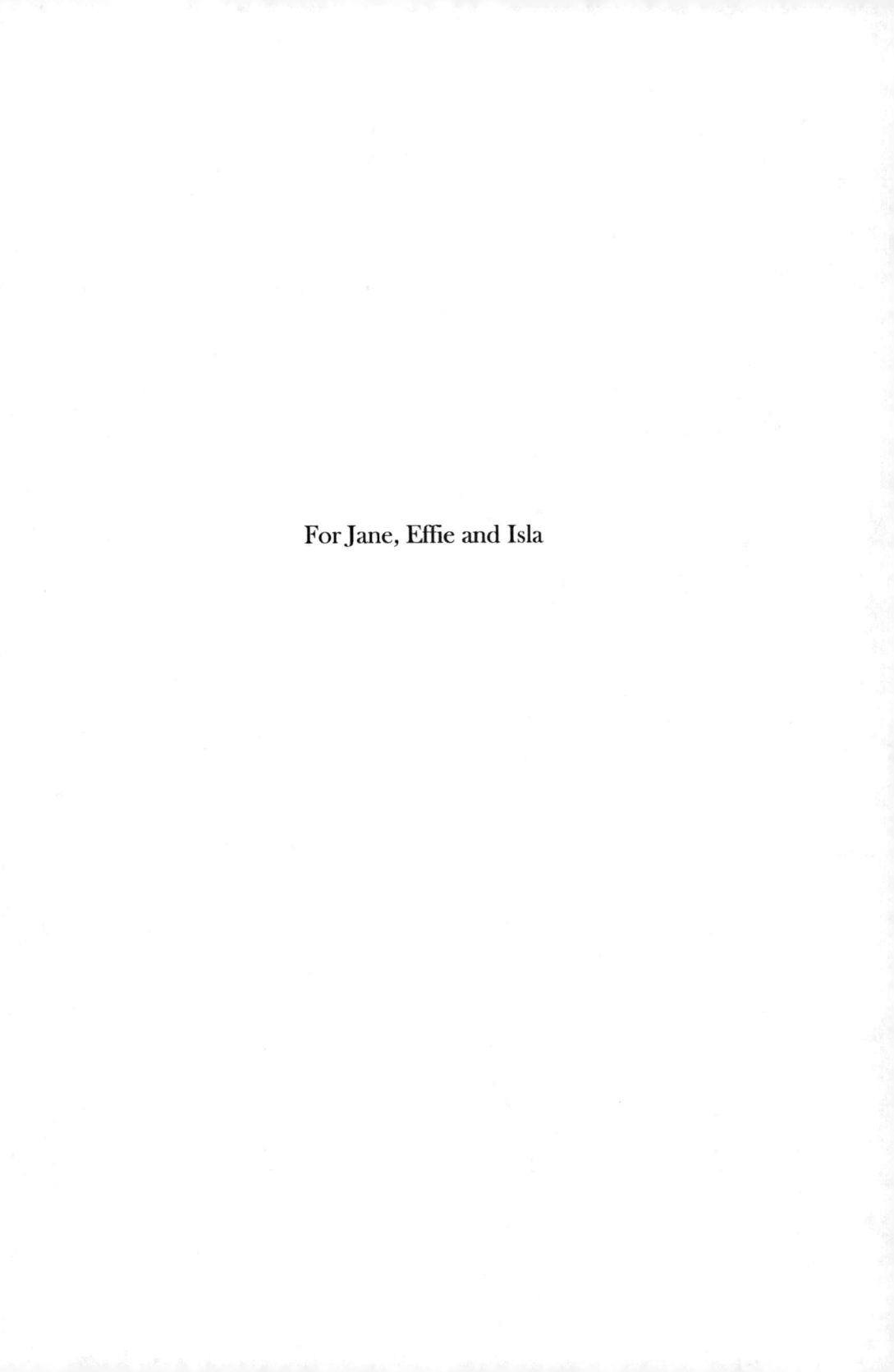

For Jane, Effie and Isla

Mountains

The white Mazda was touching one hundred and seventy-five kilometers per hour and accelerating when it entered the tunnel. It had been weaving dangerously between lanes ever since they had picked it up and the driver had made no attempt to stop despite their lights and sirens.

The Guardia Alfa Romeo, unable to keep pace, had given up the chase and instead radioed ahead for assistance before following at a safe distance.

Further towards Malaga the motorway was being cleared, exits blocked and stingers deployed to try and bring the car safely to a halt.

The exact point at which the driver lost control was not immediately clear but, at some point, the car had touched the safety barrier in the tunnel and barrel-rolled across the carriageway before hitting the central reservation and bursting into flames.

Miraculously, no one save the driver was injured but he, or she, was dead, very dead. The Alfa reached the scene just in time to see the petrol tank explode turning the wreckage into an inferno with the body trapped inside. The flames were too fierce for the officers to approach so they watched and waited for the *bombaderos* to arrive.

As their fire extinguishers went to work and all the combustible material was consumed by the flames an eerie quiet descended on the scene only punctuated by the occasional crackle of the police radio.

* * *

The lynx was a survivor. He had learned to keep away from humans, even those that raised him. He preferred the scrublands where rabbits could be found. Food was scarce in the forest but it was a good place to hide – hide from the humans.

He had smelled them coming on the breeze before they arrived – the humans with their noisy machines. As night fell they went away and the pulse of the forest resumed – but they were back with the morning sunlight. He settled down to watch.

From his vantage point, he could see the clearing where the machines were parked and the track that led to the car park higher up the mountain. He watched as the slightly built figure left his car and began to walk down the track, stopping periodically to take pictures.

The lynx was cautious. He understood that humans were a particularly devious kind of opponent. Just last year he had narrowly avoided a large net that they had set to catch him. Prudence told him that the best course of action was to wait and watch what these were up to.

The fallow deer was grazing from the low branches. There was precious little food to be had in the summer months and she was making the most of the cool of the morning to take as much energy on board as possible.

The lynx was well aware that he had not been seen. Normally a deer would be too big to tackle but this one was a juvenile. The problem was that it was grazing close to the track. To take her he would have to get much too close to the humans – but it would mean eating well for a week.

* * *

There was something about mountains – all mountains. The rarity of the atmosphere; the fragrance of the pines; the carpet of needles accumulated over centuries all added to a sense of permanence.

The mountains had always been there. Growing up in Pamplona, the Pyrenees had been the main focus of attention and recreation for the first ten years of Rojo's life and always, since then, when the pressure was on, the closest mountains were where he would go to release the pressure.

The intervening years had treated him well. He was fit mentally and physically and, although he needed glasses for reading, at the age of forty-five he was in good shape. He had even retained his youthful appearance and only now was a freckle of grey beginning to appear in his thick black hair.

From an early age, he had understood that the brain is there to be used. A junior chess champion at thirteen, he had gone on to take leading honours in his bar examinations and after a while in private practice, had become the youngest ever judge appointed.

Thinking critically had been both a blessing in the advancement of his career and a curse. He was never free of it. If he looked at a painting he saw the brush strokes and the pigments used to create it. If he watched a film he found himself analysing the shots and settings used.

Of course, this was incredibly useful when examining potentially criminal activity but sometimes he longed to just accept things for what they were rather than look for the patterns and hierarchies underpinning them.

In recent years he had taken a camera with him whenever he visited, initially for snapshots, but as he had grown in

3

confidence, to record his love of the wild things that live there. Photographing animals afforded no time to think, only to shoot and analyse the results later. The mountains were a fertile source of good pictures.

"But these are not real mountains" he muttered to himself as he trudged along the valley "only foothills". This, his first trip to the south in many years, had proved particularly stressful. What started as a fact-finding mission had turned into a full-scale political battle. Worse, he was fighting with people who should know better than to challenge the authority vested in him.

Initially, the locals had been affable enough, eager to indulge this interloper from Madrid with information but, as time wore on, one by one, they clammed up.

"It is as if it dawned on them that they had something to hide" Baltasar, his senior investigator, had hit the nail on the head as they left the municipal offices after a frustrating day.

The brief passed to Rojo had been quite specific – investigate allegations of civic corruption going back over many years. The file history showed that it had been passed around various departments within the administration without any concrete action ever being taken – a sure sign that it was too hot to handle.

"A hospital pass." was Baltasar's typically blunt assessment. "They want us to fail. We just have to prove them wrong."

He ran over the facts of the case in his mind. It was clear from the building records that there had been numerous instances of permits being granted for the construction of leisure complexes outside the normal zoning rules. On the face of it, these had been legally, if not morally, correct as they were usually granted

4

at the discretion of the local mayor on the grounds of economic benefit.

Every time it had happened the environmental lobby had been up in arms about the encroachment upon rare habitats and the increasing urban sprawl but their protests had gone nowhere. Similarly, several attempts to investigate at a regional level had petered out.

A common pattern seemed to run through these developments – in almost every case the main developer had gone bust leaving the site to be picked up for a song by a procession of offshore companies that were proving difficult to unravel.

Throughout all these developments one name had been prominent – Mijas – initially as head of planning then as mayor. There was no obvious link between him and the failed developers or the successful ones but that would be the point upon which the case turned.

Mijas was a rich man in his own right having made his money from a string of hotels around the country. He had been feted for turning around the economy of the city and worked the lecture circuit spouting forth wise words on development to all who would listen. He was also a rising star in *Partido Popular* which made him even more dangerous and a target for the left-wing.

What was less clear was where the impetus to investigate had originated. Politics played a key role, of that he was in no doubt, but was it the left or the right in the driving seat?

Rojo knew all about politics. He was acutely aware that his rapid rise had ruffled plenty of feathers amongst those who saw their position as a sinecure and placed great value on seniority. He also knew from Baltasar that his nickname within the hierarchy was *Chucho Ingles* – the English mongrel – both a disparaging reference to his English grandmother and an indication of the contempt in which he and his fellow investigators were held.

Based in the Salamanca district, away from the incestuous milieu of the Madrid-based judiciary, he was able to keep his distance. As an investigating judge, he could afford to ride out the petty jealousies and entrenched opposition that came with that apartness. In theory, at least he worked directly for the King. He had arrived and was there for the long haul - and they all knew it.

Yet the progress of this investigation went against all his instincts and experience. Normally, he liked to sit back and assemble a cast-iron case through detailed analysis before acting. In this situation, because the investigation was public knowledge, he had been obliged to show his hand early and make visible, noisy enquiries.

"It is what they expect us to do," said Baltasar "Send in Toro to flush out the birds. They will be waiting for us."

Their enquiries so far had identified that there was going to be a dinner party for three of their suspects at *El Panorama,* a restaurant up in the Sierras, this evening. Maybe that would reveal more information.

He stopped dead. His photographer's eye had spotted the deer standing motionless – camouflaged against the trees. It was a small doe, probably a youngster. Taking care not to make any sudden moves, he raised the Canon slowly until he had a perfect shot. He adjusted the long lens to sharpen the focus on the creature that had resumed tugging on a small bush.

The deer stopped eating and raised its head uneasily. Something was not right. Rojo readjusted his focus to the trees and his heart stopped. There, absolutely still, yet also focused on the small deer was the unmistakable profile of a lynx.

It was incredibly rare to find a lynx in the wild, especially this far south – still rarer to see one about to tackle as large a prey as a deer. Rojo's shutter whirred almost silently – taking frame after frame as the lynx steadied itself to pounce.

The noise of the chainsaw shattered the peace, reverberating around. Whole flocks of birds rose in unison as Rojo cursed. He watched as the deer disappeared at speed. The lynx too was gone. He searched the edge of the trees with his telephoto lens but there was no sign that it had ever been there.

As he walked back down the valley the quiet was interrupted by the continued whine of more than one saw. Closer to the road he watched as a team of men in yellow hard hats removed the vegetation systematically, preparing the ground for construction of some kind.

Had he not left his phone in the car, Rojo would have called the Guardia to come and check their permits, but that was the point, he wanted to be away from his phone to think. A task that was proving fruitless in the face of this vandalism.

He took a picture of the truck from which the gang was being directed. He could see the back of the sign delineating the start of the national park. Whatever they were doing needed special permissions to take place on protected land.

He made a mental note to ask Baltasar. He would find out what was going on.

* * *

The motorway was closed for much of the day as a forensic team combed the tunnel for evidence. The closure meant that all the surrounding roads were congested and Rojo could feel his frustration growing as he crawled back to the villa. "So much for a relaxing morning", he muttered to himself as the traffic ground to a halt again.

CCTV showed the Mazda stopping on a slip road at the junction before the tunnel. A figure could be seen getting out of the car then leaning into the driver's door for some time before the car drove off suddenly out onto the motorway. The figure was then picked up by a red Seat just on the very edge of the camera's range. Neither the figure nor the car could be identified.

Given the charred state of the body, the autopsy was difficult but threw up several surprises. The first was that, given the amount of cocaine and whisky consumed, the driver had been able to get in the car – let alone drive it.

The second was that his right foot had been attached to the accelerator pedal with some kind of tape. Apart from his sex, identification was impossible and would have to rely upon dental records and DNA.

Full English

Sharon woke before the alarm. Outside she could hear the irritating whine of an electric truck making deliveries of milk. Mickey was snoring peacefully at her side. How he managed to sleep so soundly was a mystery to her. For a man with a million schemes and wheezes to part people from their money, he had no conscience at all.

Nor, she liked to think, did she, but she knew she was wrong – her job did worry her. Despite outward appearances, she slept only fitfully and often woke with a start, heart racing and in a hot sweat. It wasn't the prospect of getting caught – she could deal with that. It was her mother. Illogical or not it seemed like her mother was being punished for Sharon's misdeeds.

It had started years ago. She had been seeing Mickey for some time when she took him to see her parents. They had a nice family afternoon and Mickey had been charming to everyone but before they left her dad had taken her to one side.

"Be very careful" he said, "He is very glib and very plausible but there is a good chance he is a villain." She had dismissed it at the time as him just being over-protective but it was almost the last thing he ever said to her. That night he keeled over with a massive heart attack.

Her mother had been bereft. Sharon's father had been the rock upon which the family had been built. With her sister living in Australia, it fell on Sharon to keep things together. She gave up her job in London and moved to a flat close to the family home to look after her mother.

Mickey had been a star – supportive when it was needed and invisible too when that was required. When the money began to

9

get tight he had given her a job working with him and it soon became apparent just how right her dad had been. Still, Mickey enchanted her mother and his charm alongside love and stability were what she needed as she recovered slowly from the shock.

Thinking back, her mother's memory had been getting worse for years. Her father would make a joke of it and do his best to fill in for the lapses and repeated questions, covering it up. Since his death, the problem had become much worse, particularly her short-term memory. Mickey put it down to the grief but they both suspected the worse.

One day, three weeks ago, her mother was reading the paper about the sentencing of a fraudster when she broke down. In tears, she had said, "What will become of me when you go to prison?"

Sharon made light of it and, as usual with Alzheimer's, her mother had forgotten all about it very quickly but it had chilled her to the bone. Again, Mickey had been kindness itself and had helped her arrange for carers to start visiting but it remained in her memory, nagging away at her attempts to sleep.

* * *

The guards tie seemed the most appropriate. It's navy and maroon stripes offsetting his dark blue Jermyn Street suit and black brogues. He checked the matching cufflinks and set off downstairs. The breakfast room was set for the whole family and as he arrived his plate of scrambled egg and smoked salmon appeared. He poured himself a cup of the black Javanese coffee that he had imported especially.

Ivana Sanderson remained silent until she was spoken to. She knew that her husband preferred quiet at the breakfast table while he gathered his thoughts for the day.

"Anything special planned for today?" he asked conversationally.

"Not really. The girls have a riding lesson in the morning and I will probably take the opportunity to go for a massage."

"How are they getting on? I hope you insist on them wearing their helmets."

"It is drummed into them. Besides, they only ride ponies at their age."

He finished his coffee and checked his watch. "The car will be here soon. I will ring you this evening to catch up."

He checked the tie in the tall mirror in the hall. It wouldn't do for it to be anything other than correctly tied and straight. He had a meeting of the investment committee to attend when he reached the office and they would be expecting him to look the part as well as displaying his usual blend of quiet competence and nervelessness.

Despite the early hour, his mobile phone rang as it did every morning when he was at home. Personal Assistant to the Managing Director of an investment fund was a twenty-four hour a day job and Jasmine was exceptionally good at it. A ring of the doorbell indicated that his car had arrived and he pecked Ivana on the cheek before striding off, all the while listening to Jasmine on the phone.

Ivana was under no illusions about Jasmine Oh. Derek spent most of the week in their flat in St James and she was certain that, amongst other services, Jasmine kept him warm at night.

She was comfortable with that. It was the price she paid for a nice house, a healthy allowance and two beautiful daughters. One day perhaps, when she tired of Derek, she would take them back to Kyiv but that was a long way off.

Today, once she had dropped the girls off at the riding school, she had an appointment with her masseur who provided a full range of very personal services himself.

* * *

Sharon fried bacon and eggs for Mickey's breakfast.

"By the way," he said between mouthfuls "I am meeting the money this lunchtime over towards Midhurst so I won't be in until later. We have a clean pair of hands coming from the jobcentre this morning. He needs to be interviewed and employed if he is suitable. Can you handle that?"

"What is he being paid?" she queried

"It is a Government scheme. They pay half so offer him minimum wage plus a couple of quid, standard bonus based on sales. You know the rest."

The front door banged shut and she heard Mickey drive off. This was the time she hated most of all – when she was alone in the house. She tried to tell herself that, after all, these people knew the risk they would be taking by buying off-plan in a foreign country. When she tried to wheedle more information out of Mickey he had clammed up.

"There are things it is better that you don't know" was all he said but she had overheard snatches of telephone calls that made her fear the worse. The risk that the clients would lose their deposits was more likely to be a racing certainty.

At times like this, she missed her father. She had no one she could discuss it with. She had tried searching the internet for information and had come up with a Spanish development company that had made a speciality of buying up bankrupt schemes and building them out. She had also uncovered that Estados Developments was in its third incarnation, having gone bust twice before.

Putting two and two together it was not difficult to see what was happening. Even more worrying was that if she could work it out – so could anyone. No wonder anyone with Spanish connections was weeded out.

The phone interrupted her thought process. It was Jana, her mother's carer. Her mother was becoming increasingly fractious and Jana kept Sharon in touch with the latest problems every day.

"Morning" Sharon could always tell a lot from Jana's tone. This was a routine call rather than an emergency "How is she?"

"She had a good night. Only the usual toilet problems. Did you remember that today we have to take her for her MRI scan?"

"Damn" Sharon had forgotten all about it. "What time is the appointment?"

"We have to be at the hospital at two-thirty. It will take about an hour in the machine. I can wait with her if you like but she prefers you are there to keep her calm."

That meant that she would be out of the office all afternoon. Sharon cursed inwardly. "No problem Jana, I'll see you at the house at about half-past twelve" She tipped her half-drunk mug of coffee down the sink and reached for her car keys. She would need to get her skates on this morning if she was at the hospital all afternoon.

* * *

Butler hadn't slept well. The thought of his presentation to the security committee had acted as an impediment – careers had begun and ended on such occasions. The slides had been finalised for ages and he was a senior officer in command of his brief but still he saw each hour go by - dozing fitfully in between.

The idea of an early morning run was enough on its own to sharpen his instincts and clear his head. He pounded his way across Brick Lane past the Mosque and Spitalfields market into the heart of the City. He was surprised by how many people were up and about already despite it being barely light.

The temples of money were lit up as the institutions of finance cranked into action. The presentation was about money flows and there was no better place to observe them in action than the City of London.

He dodged a dustman wheeling out a large bin of empties before the dustcart raised it and shook out the contents with a deafening crash.

"Someone's been enjoying themselves" he shouted over the din as their paths crossed. Coming up to London Bridge he looked upriver towards Blackfriars Bridge. The case of Calvi, the Italian banker found hanging from the bridge, had been one of his case studies at the academy and had piqued his interest in institutional corruption.

He paused for a breather and looked back at the forest of skyscrapers. There had been a time, within his memory, when London was a low-rise place – now it was high-rise and getting higher. He wondered how much of the money sloshing around was truly legitimate. Taking that thought he continued with his run.

* * *

He was waiting when Sharon arrived. "Can I help you?" He looked about twelve years old.

"I am Dominic Sharp. The jobcentre sent me."

Sharon looked him up and down. "How old are you Dominic?"

"Twenty-three – but I know I look younger."

"Have you ever done anything like this before?"

"I worked in a call centre while I was at University which is sort of relevant because I was talking to members of the public."

"Really? What were you saying?"

"Not much. Mostly they would just put the phone down. Sometimes they would swear first."

Sharon smiled "Do you know what we are doing?"

"Selling apartments they said at the jobcentre."

She smiled again "Technically right, but tactically wrong. We are selling a lifestyle that involves owning an apartment in Spain."

"So we are emphasising all the good things about living in the sun to people who are fed-up with the rain."

She was beginning to like him "Exactly. Those of them who have the means to do something about it. What do you think?"

"I think I could do that"

"I think you could too" She could see him going down very well with the seniors. "My name is Sharon. I am the manager here. However, I don't know about the full terms of your employment – that will have to wait until the boss gets in."

"I assumed that it would be minimum wage"

"Let's assume that it is, but it might be more than that. Would you be OK to start, like, now?"

He nodded "Strike while the iron is hot"

"I have to take my mum to the hospital this afternoon and the boss is out all day so I desperately need someone to hold the fort. So, I will find you a workstation and run through the script with you."

Malaga

There were many reasons why Baltasar hated being away from home. Top of the list was uncomfortable beds. He had woken with a stiff back from the bed in the villa and his temper had not been improved by the antics of his housemates. Rio had left early for the gym, Toro had gone for a run and even the boss, Judge Rojo, had gone for a drive.

It was not as if he had anything against running or the gym per se. It was just that he didn't wish to participate. Over the years he had put on a few kilos but he felt that it added a certain gravitas to his role as Chief Inspector – as did the grey beard that he had grown to disguise his double chin.

Fortunately, the staff seemed immune to the excesses of physical activity and served him his breakfast alongside a mug of hot black coffee. He thought it had been a secret between his wife and him but the cook seemed aware of his weakness for *Tostada y Jamon* with tomato and a hint of garlic. He had to admit, she had done a good job.

Hopefully, they wouldn't have to stay in Malaga too long. It was only so that they could take statements from all those linked to the alleged crimes. He doubted that there would be any arrests this early in the investigation but he lived in hope that someone would come forward and confess to everything so they could go back to Madrid.

He enjoyed the operational aspects of an enquiry. That was why, two years ago, he had opted for the job of running Judge Rojo's investigation team rather than a desk job in Madrid despite the promotion that came attached. He had a free hand to build the team and felt that he had selected well.

Toro had been a rising star in the national force but his bluntness had not gone down well with the sophisticated Madrid elite and he had been in danger of being sidelined.

Dos Rios had always been something of a maverick with a tendency to act first and think through the consequences afterwards but Baltasar had always known her as a conscientious and rigorous investigator. Others made jibes about her sexuality but, as he had been obliged to point out on many occasions, she had bigger balls than most of her detractors. She was a risky pick for the team as she was under a disciplinary cloud for assaulting a suspect during an arrest. As Baltasar knew full well, resisting an arrest by Helena Dos Rios could be a dangerous business and he liked the edge that gave the team.

Food and coffee had done their work and he felt more at ease with the world. As the perspiring figure of Toro arrived outside the front door, Baltasar went in search of another *Tostada*.

* * *

She found that it helped if she had a face in her mind's eye as she pounded the punchbag causing it to swing and sway. In the zone, she danced around it, punching hard until she felt the trainer's hand on her arm.

"Slow down champ. I think he has taken enough damage. Besides, your footwork is all to shit. You box like that and you will end up on the floor."

"I don't box. If I fight, generally they don't get that close."

"Yes. I heard about the karate thing."

"The boxing helps me work it out."

"Sure. Be more measured rather than just hitting out. Stay on your toes and pick the hits. "

Helena Dos Rios pulled off the boxing gloves and turned to go before unleashing a full roundhouse kick at the punchbag. The niggles that she had woken up with had been replaced by an icy calm.

"Better?" asked the coach.

"Much better," said Rio

Later, as the shower hosed the adrenaline out of her system, Rio reflected on how these early morning sessions were good for her. She had been recommended to the gym by the psychiatrist allocated to her after she had injured one Javier Hernandes badly while he was trying to flee the scene of a murder. "Of course," she told herself "Nobody cared that he was roughed up."

Many of her colleagues would have done the same – but she was identified by the karate kick with which she had disabled him and the press had got hold of it. They managed to turn Hernandes from a drug-peddling scumbag into a helpless victim of police brutality. Something had to be seen to be done so she served a couple of weeks suspension and had to sign up to an anger management strategy.

She had also been transferred to a backroom position to keep her out of the public eye. She had considered chucking it all in at that point but her old boss, Baltasar, was setting up a new team working directly for a Judge and he asked for her. The municipal police breathed a sigh of relief and seconded her immediately before she caused any more trouble.

She didn't normally bear grudges but Javier Hernandes face was the one she used when boxing.

* * *

Running wasn't a normal state for Toro but he understood that, however unnatural it seemed, it was doing him good physically and mentally. He found that once he had established a rhythm he reached almost a trance fairly quickly and, once there, he was able to think rationally about whatever the problems besetting him were.

The plan was to run from the villa across the motorway then back down the hill where the motorway went into a tunnel. His playlist ran for exactly fifty-five minutes which was just about the length of the run - if he stepped out.

He was quickly into the groove. A few days in Malaga was a few days away from his family. Fortunately, his wife was on top of childcare and his sons wouldn't miss him during the week but he hoped that he would be back in Madrid by the weekend.

The case was a tricky one involving the sale of building permits in restricted areas. Toro would have preferred something simpler like a bank robbery but he understood that theft took many forms.

As he pounded over the motorway bridge he didn't notice the white Mazda hurtling along the road and *Firework* drowned out the howl of its engine.

He felt the explosion in the tunnel rather than heard it but it was enough to stop him in his tracks. He watched as the Guardia arrived and cordoned off the entrance to the tunnel then, unable to contribute, jogged gently back to the villa.

Surveillance

Rojo shifted his weight from his left buttock to his right. The seat was just too hard to sustain a two-hour vigil and this was getting on for three. "They must have a lot to discuss" he murmured, almost to himself.

"Rio says they are drinking coffee and expensive brandy." Baltasar's attention to the viewfinder of the Canon never wavered. "They should be leaving soon."

"I hope so, my backside is numb and I need to pee"

Toro looked at Rojo in the back seat and Baltasar, crouched over the camera. Ever since he was a small boy he had always wanted to be a policeman and as a man, he had proved to be quite good at arresting criminals. He enjoyed the action, the cut and thrust of the battle with criminality. So good had he become that, to his horror, he was seconded to join Rojo's investigation team in Madrid. Since that day two years had passed. Two years of sitting, watching and, very occasionally, acting.

What was a man like Judge Jesus Rojo doing sitting in a nondescript Nissan in a restaurant car park at 2 am? He asked himself. This was a man at the top of his game. The youngest ever investigating judge. Head of the anti-corruption team. A confidant of Ministers, hated by the old establishment and yet still a hands-on investigator prepared to pitch in. Toro admired him greatly - as did all the team – and that made up for nights like this.

* * *

Rio fired off another burst of shots using the small Nikon. From her position in the kitchen, she could see all six men, but two of them had their backs to her. She recognised Mijas, the local Mayor, from the case notes. On a separate table, two large men sat watchfully, clearly on guard. She didn't know the others but Anya, the waitress, had confirmed that one of them was an Englishman.

This wasn't unusual, many English had made their homes in the south of Spain, but this one made her uneasy. It surprised her that, despite being in the middle of a foreign country, on Mijas home turf, the Englishman controlled the table. When he was serious, they listened. When he laughed, they laughed. There was an edge about him that Rio didn't like.

The smiling waitress pushed the plate of torta towards her. She wavered again. Taking a fork Anya cut off a piece and proffered it to her. Rio looked into her hazel eyes and opened her mouth slightly. The sweetness of the honey alone made the game worthwhile.

"Where are you from Anya?"

"Bratislava, Slovakia" She spoke Spanish with a breathless accent that Rio found irresistible.

"What time does your shift finish?"

* * *

The restaurant sat high on the edge of the mountains and Bessie was finding the climb a bit of a strain. Mary changed down furiously as the ascent became slower and slower.

"Cameras primed for action?" She nodded. "I want some answers tonight" Greg peered out of the windscreen, bright-

22

eyed. "He won't answer my calls and won't meet me to discuss anything. Let's see if he likes me door-stepping him."

* * *

On cue, the bodyguards left the restaurant. Mijas moved his chair back and stood up. Rio's attention was held by Anya's pouting lips and comfortable body but she saw the motion out of the corner of her eye.

"End of meal" she hissed into her microphone.

"They are coming" relayed Baltasar, his grip tightening on the camera. Rio watched as Mijas signed the bill with a flourish and put down some notes on the table.

Three black Mercedes drew up outside the main door as the men emerged from the restaurant. Baltasar's camera whirred and clicked constantly as the two bodyguards leapt out and opened the passenger doors. The man Rojo recognised as Judge Hector Diamante climbed into the back seat of the first car which pulled away almost immediately. The Head of Planning, Parador, chatted to the bodyguards while Mijas attention was entirely upon the unknown Englishman.

The old campervan looked spectacularly out of place at it spluttered and coughed its way into the car park narrowly avoiding Diamante's Mercedes as it sped away. It looked for all the world as though it had been hand-painted in emulsion. Artistic butterflies fluttered up both doors. "What in the name of God is this?" muttered Baltasar, still shooting as the VW ground to a halt in front of the other vehicles.

The bodyguards watched suspiciously as a young man with unruly hair stepped out of the van and approached the car, microphone extended. "Greg Matthews, Costa Enquirer" he began. "I would like to ask Mayor Mijas a few questions..."

Mijas pushed the Englishman into the back seat of one car while Parador jumped into the second. As one, the two cars moved forward towards the rusty old VW blocking their path.

"...about the development of apartments in a designated area of outstanding natural beauty inside a National Park".

The rear window of Mijas car opened soundlessly. "Would you be so kind as to move your vehicle" said Mijas without a hint of menace. "It is late and my men would like to go home."

"Mayor Mijas. Greg Matthews Costa Enquirer, I would like to ask.." Mijas held up his hand "I think you will agree that even a Mayor is allowed time off for a quiet dinner with friends. I am not answering any questions this evening. Make an appointment to see me at my office and I will speak to you there. Now could you please move your van."

"Your office seems reluctant to talk to me, Mr Mayor. I just want to know about illegal permits being granted to build in the National Park"

Mijas smiled. "There will be no illegal building in the National Park Mr Matthews. Now I repeat..."

The flash from the small camera lit up the Mayor's face as it turned from a smile to a snarl. "No photographs. Move that heap of shit before we push it out of the way". The Mercedes revved intimidatingly as Mary slipped Bessie into reverse and pulled back slowly.

"Deal with him. Take the camera" Mijas shouted as the cars roared off.

Matthews began to retreat as Huertas and Caballo moved in. "I am an accredited journalist," he said with a tremor in his voice. " I am ...." The first blow hit him in the solar plexus as the bodyguards set about their task with a will. In an instant, Matthews was on the floor taking kicks to the body.

"I am afraid, Ingles, that you never learned to keep your fucking nose out of business that doesn't concern you" Huertas prised the camera out of Matthews grasp. He examined the controls.

"Nice camera. I think that this button here deletes the pictures and this one here ejects the memory card. There we are. Now it is a useless camera. What a pity". Matthews vomited.

The vomit splashed over Huertas' brown Loake brogues and up the leg of his dark blue Armani suit. He looked at Matthews with disgust.

He always took pride in his appearance. Just because his job involved getting his hands dirty he always felt that it paid dividends to look smart. He had bought this suit in Milan while on holiday with his girlfriend last year and his shoes were English, bought in a shop in Marbella.

"You piece of shit." He aimed a kick at Matthew's head.

"Enough". Rojo nodded to Toro who leapt from the Nissan. Striding into the middle of the car park he fired his gun into the air. Huertas and Caballo froze at the sound of the shot, then fled in different directions leaving the bloodied, moaning Matthews on the floor. Toro watched the bodyguards running into the scrub then knelt beside him and inspected the damage.

"Ribs?" Matthews winced under his expert touch. "Yes".

Mary emerged from the campervan as Toro helped the reporter to his feet. "Good job you were passing." Toro avoided her stare.

"Police?" Toro nodded sheepishly.

"What were you doing here?"

"Looking into some traffic offences - Take him to hospital. They will need to bandage him up."

Mary nodded. "It seems a bit heavy-handed for traffic offences...."

Toro turned his attention to Bessie. "We have been made aware of some unsafe vehicles being used in the area..."

Mary pushed the groaning Matthews into the passenger seat. "I think I had better take him to the hospital"

"I think that is a wise course of action," said Toro.

Toro watched as the VW trundled off down the hill then turned back to the Nissan. "Do you want me to arrest the two heavies? They won't have gone far. We are in the middle of nowhere"

Rojo shook his head. "No, the less visible we are tonight the better. We have already attracted too much interest." A row of frightened faces peered out from the windows of the restaurant.

"I doubt that Toro can be invisible – they saw him quite plainly" Baltasar turned to face Rojo. "They could be useful."

Rio jogged up to the car, gun in hand. "They are both hiding in the scrub at the back of the restaurant. They will need their car to get back to town."

Rojo scratched his ear "Which car is it?"

"The red Leon, behind us"

26

"OK. Toro do you have any uniform with you?"

Toro shrugged "I have my jacket in the boot"

"Give it to Baltasar. Rio?"

"Yes, cap and jacket"

"Toro and I will head off to town. You follow us as far as the junction with the main road and park up. When they come down, stop them for speeding or something and bring them in."

* * *

Bessie was much more comfortable going downhill. As the speed increased she bounced and juddered down the badly maintained road - every movement making Matthews wince with pain. Mary leaned over and stroked his knee.

"Did you get the pictures?" he hissed through clenched teeth. "Oh Yes," said Mary "Oh yes".

* * *

Huertas watched the two cars leave the car park from behind the restaurant. They didn't look like policemen but the guy doing the shooting certainly had an impact and Huertas for one didn't want to mess with him. With much cursing, a crouching Caballo joined him behind the clump of cactus.

"They are going to the hospital with the Ingles"

"I need to go to the hospital," Caballo whined. "I have cut my knee and torn my suit"

Huertas looked at the flapping leg of the cheap imported suit and the spreading bloodstain.

"What were they doing here? Why didn't they come after us?"

"Who cares? Let's just go home and forget about it"

Huertas's eyes followed the lights of the two cars into the distance.

"OK," he said "Let's go"

Huertas was proud of his red Seat Leon. It was his first genuinely new car. Before he had always made do with second-hand, clapped-out wrecks but the Leon was the best car he had ever owned.

"Don't to bleed on the seat." He drove at speed down the mountain road as Caballo dabbed at his injured leg with a tissue.

"Here. Press on it with this". Caballo howled as the uneven surface caused the car to jolt. They swept on down the hill.

Slurry plays an important role in Spanish agriculture. It is collected and used as a genuinely organic fertiliser and spread on the fields to rejuvenate the soil. At the bottom of the hill, just where the road appeared to fork, just next to the slurry pond, Baltasar had parked blocking the road.

"Christ" shouted Huertas as he stamped on the brakes attempting to avoid a collision. The Leon missed the unmarked police car but skidded sideways into the slurry pond.

Enraged, Huertas flung open the driver's door "What the fuck do you think you are doing?"

He leapt out of the car to find himself waist-deep in the slurry. Rio could barely conceal her amusement

"Hello boys. Going somewhere nice?"

Serious Crime

Butler was coming to the end of his presentation. "The flow of funds offshore has been rising significantly over the last few years. It is difficult to quantify it exactly but conservative estimates range between fifty and sixty billion a year." The audience watched the slideshow impassively. "It is assumed that the vast majority of this is money transferred, if not generated, legally but it underlines the fact that organised criminality in the UK is generating more cash than ever before and exporting it out of our jurisdiction in ever greater amounts. It is hard not to draw the conclusion that these transfers are either being instigated or facilitated by institutional involvement in the process.

It is also worth remembering that this is an international problem, not just a national one. It has become much harder to coordinate and control cross border criminality since we lost access to the pan-European databases held by the European Union and, while there may be co-operation at the level of individual officers in different countries, official collaboration is limited and sclerotic. They move very quickly, we do not and that has to change."

"Thank you, Jack, for that summary." As the lights came back on the group of people around the table re-engaged. Craddock continued. "That is the background to the establishment of this task force. We have representatives here from Fraud, Cyber and all the other specialist branches of the force. Our sister organisations at Her Majesties Revenue and Customs and the Border Force are also represented. The purpose of today's meeting is really for you all to communicate, network and generally talk to each other. The criminal fraternity is getting smarter and smarter. We need to match that degree of intelligence and it starts with communication."

"What about the international aspect of this?" The question came from the only uniformed person around the table "We can do a lot within the UK but a lot of this kind of large-scale crime is often initiated elsewhere.

You make no mention of the flow of hooky money into the UK. We used to get tipped off by the French, for example, when anything important was going down that might affect us, now we have to ask. How can we best engage with police forces overseas?"

"A good point from HMRC. We need to communicate with police around the globe to make this initiative effective. Equally clearly, it would be impossible to sit them all around a table like this to discuss the matter.

There are top-level meetings with many forces – we have good relations with the FBI, for example - but to make this work we need the interaction to be at a local level with individual forces on a case by case basis.

Frankly, I am just as concerned that individual forces within the UK communicate routinely. Our strategy will be to embed officers within local forces to pursue particular cases and ensure that they liaise with the appropriate authorities elsewhere in the UK and internationally."

"How do we stop it getting out?" The question came from an earnest young man with long hair behind a badge saying Cybercrime. "I mean if we are after the top players they have enormous resources. If they know we are after them they will just see us off."

Craddock smiled grimly "We are under no illusion about the need to deploy resources in this area but as we are all aware, spending money speculatively is not popular politically. Nevertheless, we have Home Office guarantees underpinning our budget. As far as security is concerned Ladies and Gentlemen look around this table.

As far as you or I can see, everyone around this table is of the highest probity – at least we trust you are. You have all been vetted individually before being allocated this responsibility.

The fact of your attendance here has been classified Top Secret under the GSC as will be all the records of the meeting. You have also signed the Official Secrets Act.

This question goes to the heart of why all this is necessary. If I may quote Churchill - *Beware the sleeping dragon. For when she awakes the Earth will shake.* He was talking about China but years of inattention have allowed the dragon of organised financial criminality to grow more powerful similarly. We need to be well prepared for it to wake up.

If we are right and we uncover systemic criminality - certainly, the earth will shake as soon as the dragon becomes aware. Some of you may see this as a career-enhancing opportunity but bear in mind that if anyone of us mishandles it or lets slip anything before we are ready, be under no illusion, it could also be fatal – literally and metaphorically.

* * *

Craddock was standing by the window of his office, looking out over Canary Wharf. "It is simply statistics Jack." He said gesturing at the office blocks basking in the afternoon sun. "Just as it is almost certain, statistically, that other planets exist that

31

support life – it is certain that somewhere in this financial universe spread out in front of us there is criminality. All the data shows us that it is of a scale that, hitherto, we haven't imagined."

Jack Butler was concerned "Might that scale be just too big to handle?"

Craddock moved across to a filing cabinet. "This is the point in the old films when the senior copper gets the whisky out and offers the young detective a glass." He pulled out a bottle of spring water. "Sometimes I miss those days. Villains were villains. You knew who the good guys were and who was bad. Now it is anyone's guess"

Butler smiled "The villains all wore black hats apparently. It made them easier to spot."

Craddock took a swig from the bottle "You can take the piss all you like Jack Butler but they were good times."

"Surely you don't think that institutional wrongdoing didn't exist twenty years ago?"

"No of course not. It has existed as long as the institutions themselves but it is getting worse. I mentioned the FBI in the meeting. What I didn't say is that they identified the involvement of organised crime in their fund management industry some years ago and they have yet to root it out.

You can see why. It is far easier and more lucrative to rob people with a stroke of the pen than to kick down their doors and take their cash. There is no reason to suppose that we are any more honest over here. What worries me is that the crime itself has become ingrained in systems and operations and we won't be able to bring it to a halt without bringing the institutions themselves down. We just don't know the size and shape of what we are dealing with here. That is why I want to approach it from the ground up."

"A scoping exercise"

"Exactly. If we pick up any bad boys in the process all the better, but the real value will be in identifying some of the big players. The real problem will be hiding our investigation from the vested interests and believe me, they are everywhere."

"Are you including the home team in this?"

"Sadly yes. Already, we have evidence of political corruption, to which the response has been muted. It is safe to think that the constabulary is not immune. Because we don't know who may or may not be corrupt, we have to assume the worst. Unless they have been specifically and personally vetted we don't share information of any kind with any officer regardless of rank or seniority. The criminality will likely be protected at an extremely high level.

Depending on what we find, I suspect that any remedy that affects the integrity of some of these funds may be deemed impolitic but we will have to cross that bridge if we come to it. Secrecy, by the way, includes the very fact of our investigation. All our guys will be working undercover – you included."

"What do you have in mind?"

"The FBI brought a particular tactic to our attention. Property is one of those things whose value is determined by what people are prepared to pay for it. The mob would target blocks of apartments, move their people in and deliberately run the place down, spray it with graffiti and so on. After a while, the decent tenants move out creating vacancy and the whole downward spiral continues. At this point, the mob, in the guise of an investment fund, makes an offer for the property that reflects its shabby state. Once they own it, all the problems go away, they smarten the place up creating demand, decent tenants move back in and they sell the asset for top dollar."

Craddock picked up a file from his desk.

"We have had a team of analysts looking through the data to identify groups of transactions where this has happened. It is difficult to isolate anything suspicious because that pattern is what drives the investment industry – buy low sell high – but they usually achieve that either by investing significantly in the asset or riding the market. However, we have found a few examples that look fishy. Have a look through this and tell me what you think."

Butler read the summary pages at the front of the folder.

"Estados Developments. That is just a front surely?"

"I imagine so. They are funded by a company based in the Cayman Islands. They have a big project on the go building a couple of hundred villas plus a commercial centre in Spain.

What is interesting is that this project is funded mainly by a fund called Reichenbach, headquartered in the UK and one of the leading lights of our fund management industry I am told.

Estados has previous in this area. They have gone bust at least twice, each time they were building apartments in Spain which were then picked up by the reborn version of the company for a song.

Needless to say that any punters foolish enough to pay them a deposit lost out."

"And they are at it again?"

"Yes. They have a pop-up shop in Brighton selling villas in the new development off-plan. I do not doubt that the usual strategy will be deployed.

The real question for us though is whether Reichenbach is involved in any criminality or whether they are being duped. We strongly suspect the former.

They are under the leadership of one Derek Sanderson who features in the file.

We have made arrangements to parachute you into the local force temporarily. They have a DI vacancy which, ostensibly, you will be filling. Our involvement will be on a need to know basis so you will need to keep your wits about you.

Your contact will be Superintendent Amanda Smallbone. She is fully vetted and will make contact with you once you are in post."

"A deposit-taking scam seems like pretty small beer for us"

"And for Reichenbach too. We suspect that it is a front for serious money-laundering. It is, of course, fiendishly difficult to get any financial detail about them as they too are registered in the Cayman Islands. Ideally, we can use Estados as a gateway to find out more."

"OK. I will need access to our usual people in Fraud for example."

"No problem. You will have all the resources you need but I have to warn you that things could get quite hairy if we do manage to finger them.

Fraud has already tried and it ended badly for them. Don't underestimate your enemy would be the lesson I take from that. They can be completely ruthless when it comes to protecting themselves.

You might be forgiven for thinking that I am talking about Chicago rather than Brighton but don't hesitate to call for support, including SWAT if you think you need it. I don't need any dead heroes."

The sell

Mickey Fisher surveyed the room from the doorway. He made it twelve people. Their registration details showed him that their average age was 61, they had been married for about 30 years give or take and that the breadwinner had been employed consistently ever since leaving school.

"Ideal" he murmured to himself. There were a couple of outliers, a gay couple in their fifties betraying their wealth with plenty of bling and a couple of widows looking for a new start.

"You remind me so much of our daughter."

Sharon smiled sweetly "Thank you. That is nice"

"She lives in Spain. Her husband is Spanish" A small nervous tingle flashed across Sharon's antennae.

"Oh really? What does he do?"

"He is a lawyer. He works for a bank in Madrid"

"In Madrid?" The red warning light was on. "and you are planning to move closer to your daughter? That is nice"

A vision of her mother watching daytime TV floated into Sharon's view "When are you coming to see me?"

"Sorry, dear?"

Sharon regained her composure "Oh just listen to me! I was thinking of my mum and going to see her. I think it's really important to live as close as possible don't you? It makes life so much easier all round."

"Oh yes. Don't you think so Ron?" Ron nodded obediently

Sharon smiled again "Just like my Dad. I don't want to put you off but Aguilera is quite a long way from Madrid. Spain is a really big place. It must be four or five hours by car. You might find it is quicker from here even though it is a further distance."

"Oh that's no good is it Ron" Ron shook his head obediently.

"Oh, that is a shame" Red changed to amber. "Perhaps you son-in-law could find you somewhere closer. There is nothing like having someone you trust on the ground."

"I don't think he wants us over there at all." Ron grumbled "He wants her all to himself".

"Never mind, have another glass of Cava and watch the slideshow. You might find it interesting."

"We need to go to Asda. Don't we Ron" Ron nodded and drained his glass "Sorry to have...."

"No. It is no problem. I fully understand" Sharon ushered the couple past Mickey into the main office. "I am only glad we found out before we had gone any further. There is no point in me trying to sell you something unsuitable."

Shutting the shop door behind them she watched then walk off down Springfield Road. The warning light changed from amber to Green.

Mickey was close behind her. "Problem?"

"Not really. Son-in-law is a Spanish lawyer. I got rid of them"

Mickey kissed her on the cheek "Executive action. I like it"

"Not in the office" Sharon placed her finger on the tip of his nose and pushed him away.

* * *

"Ladies and Gentlemen if you could sit yourselves down we will make a start" The clear tones of Kevin van Vleyn rang out from the back room. The show was about to begin and the audience shuffled obligingly into the seats arranged in front of the screen. Mickey and Sharon took seats at the back.

"First of all thank you for giving up your time this afternoon. We appreciate the opportunity to tell you about a remarkable development of apartments and villas between the mountains and the sea in southern Spain. Just before we start how many of you have been to Spain?" Everyone raised their hand "Good and how many know the Costa del Sol?"

"Good. Roughly two-thirds of you. That gives me a good idea of what you already know"

Kevin sipped on a glass of water

"Let me tell you the format for this talk. First of all, I am going to tell you a bit about Estados Developments and what we do. Then I am going to show you our remarkable Aguilera development and, believe me, you will be impressed. Thirdly I am going to run you through the logistics of how you might get a piece of Aguilera and then, Ladies and Gentlemen I am going to send you away to think about what you have seen. There will be no pressure on you to sign up today – in fact, we discourage it because we realize that this is a significant commitment for you and we want you to make the right choice."

"If you have any questions – and I hope you do – you will have an opportunity to ask them at the end of the presentation"

"So, as you can see, we are Estados Developments. There is no reason why you should know about us but we have been going since the 1970's developing residential property in Spain,

Portugal and the Balearic islands. More recently we have established subsidiaries in Turkey, Bulgaria and we have an interesting project developing a ski complex in Slovenia. This shop is just the tip of a large iceberg and has been opened to give more people access to our properties. Normally, for an exclusive development such as Aguilera, we would promote the property as widely as possible. However, on this occasion, we have tightened up our marketing to an exclusive list of potential members. Believe me, this development will be very exclusive – we are pretty strict about to whom we sell to protect the existing investors. You will be delighted to hear that everyone in this room has been prequalified as suitable owners of part of Aguilera."

Kevin's eyes worked the room, meeting each couple in turn. Mickey leaned over to Sharon "He is such a smooth bastard. They all feel special now" he whispered.

"Aguilera – the Eagles Nest - is a development like no other. Set between the mountains and the sea in an area of outstanding beauty yet easily accessible from the motorway network and Malaga airport. As you can see from these pictures it is a special place and we hope to complement it with some special properties."

The screen showed spectacular valleys and mountain crags, teeming with wildlife.

"Over the next two years, we will be building three apartment blocks and just fifty-four villas in the first phase of the development"

The wildlife was replaced with pictures of happy people, relaxing around a pool

"All apartments offer balconies or terraces, each apartment block has an on-site concierge and a fitness suite that incorporates an indoor plunge pool; villas all come with three or four luxury bedrooms and bags of external space for entertaining or just relaxing.

The site itself will be landscaped around water with plenty of tree cover to offer shade. As you will know temperatures can get pretty high in this area in the summer and the design objective is to provide an oasis environment."

Pictures of cool shade with more happy people. Sharon's thoughts drifted again to her mother, trapped in the house by her arthritis. She could do with some of those high temperatures.

Watching the audience, enraptured by Kevin's photographs she could see how attractive this illusion could be. But it was an illusion, she knew that. This was just a means of separating people from their savings, as Mickey had put it, and she was up to her neck in it.

"When you buy a stylish and contemporary new home at Aguilera you could take advantage of many benefits and services that can save you time, money and stress, including our exclusive warranties on fixtures and fittings.

With no language problems, upwards chain or structural survey to worry about, we will ensure that you will enjoy a seamless and stress-free purchase at Aguilera."

A seamless transfer of cash from your savings account would be a better description thought Sharon and that funded her new BMW and clothes and her mother's care.

She looked around the room again these were trout being played by the master fisherman Kevin. He tickled them under their bellies and they loved every minute of it. They deserved to be taken.

"Five hundred k in this room I reckon" Mickey whispered in her ear "Look forward to spending some of it"

Kevin had moved on to the small print that all sounded so plausible. We are on your side he was saying. Trust us with your money.

"Now this is the part of the morning where you get to ask all those questions that you have been bursting to ask. Before we start is everyone OK to continue or would you like a comfort break?" A ripple of assent moved around the room. "OK the loos are at the back – we'll kick off again in ten minutes."

Mickeys phone rang and he stretched and stood up "I have to take this," he said, "are you OK to close up here?" Sharon nodded. They walked back into the shop together.

"How hard to get are we playing?"

"I expect a couple of signings today. Make it seem like you are doing them a big favour though and make sure the others know that they are getting first choice on the villas."

"We should convert four or five out of the twelve"

"And you have already lost one of them. Your team are going to have to pull all the stops out. I need to go. I am supposed to be in Midhurst by one-thirty."

Sharon watched as Mickey cruised out of the shop with a cheery smile. She turned back to the presentation.

One of the widows opened "How do I know my money is safe?" Kevin smiled. "Good question. Look I understand that Spanish developers don't have a good reputation and some horror stories are going around about people buying property off-plan then losing their deposit."

Knowledgeable heads in the audience nodded.

"It happened to my sister. She invested big time in a proposed development in Alicante, despite my advice. When it failed to get the necessary permissions she had a lot of trouble getting her money back."

"Well rest assured it won't happen to you. Projects in Spain fail for two main reasons. Firstly money: some developers rely entirely upon deposits taken to fund the construction. That is fine in a booming market but if things cool down – suddenly there is a cash flow crisis and they can't afford to build.

I have seen that happen perhaps three times over the past twenty years – all of which have been heavily reported on by the media. The fact that we are talking to you today represents a conscious strategy on our part.

This time last year the proposal was that we construct Aguilera speculatively and then sell the properties at a premium price. Typically, when that happens the Germans and the Swedes snap them up before anyone over here gets a look in.

We didn't think that was fair so we decided to sell Aguilera off-plan in the UK only. The key point though is that we have the funding in place to build out the complex without resorting to any deposits.

When you pay over your fifteen per cent we invest it in an escrow account where it earns interest, not for us – but you. All the interest earned comes off the final bill so you never lose out."

The knowledgeable heads were nodding again.

"I mentioned that there were two reasons" Kevin was on a roll

"The second reason projects fail is improper documentation of ownership and permissions – this is what tripped up my sister.

This a complex area and, while we use our expertise to help you if we can, we recommend that you employ your own solicitor with the correct accreditation and expertise.

We have a list of these to help you choose. You don't have to pick from the list, you can use your solicitor if you like but these are people that we know are experienced in the area of land transfer and who will provide you with value for money.

Ladies and Gentlemen. I have kept you here for a long time this morning. I hope you have found it informative. As I said at the outset we recommend that you go away and sleep on it before you make any decisions.

By all means, stay and have another glass of wine. Look at the models and discuss things with one of our representatives. Thank you for your time."

Kevin bowed as the applause rang out around the room.

* * *

It took the best part of an hour to clear the shop of potential purchasers by which time they had two couples signed up and another four on the brink. Sharon was clearing away the glasses when a couple that she recognised from a previous session appeared in the sales area.

"Mr and Mrs Kenton isn't it?" she asked speculatively "How can I help?"

Mrs Kenton looked tearful and he was red-faced, presumably as a result of an argument between them. "We paid a deposit last week on a villa at Aguilera"

"I remember - a type B with its own pool. As I recall Plot 27 wasn't it?"

"Yes it was"

"I am impressed with my own memory. What can I do for you today"?

"Well. The thing is... we want our money back."

Sharon had not encountered this situation before and was genuinely surprised.

"I am sorry to hear that. What made you change your minds?"

"Her son" Mr Kenton grumbled, "He thinks it is a bad idea and what he says goes."

"Oh dear" commiserated Sharon "With big decisions like these it is always a good idea to get your family on board. Nevertheless, I am sure that there will be no problem returning your money."

"See," Mrs Kenton said, "I told you. The thing is my son is a solicitor and he says that we might lose our money. He insisted that we cancel the agreement."

"Well, as we explained, your money is protected but I can see that it is causing friction between you and your son and that is the last thing we want to do."

"I told him it was protected but he wouldn't have it."

"Do you want to discuss it with him further? He is welcome to come down and talk to me so I can explain the safeguards."

Mr Kenton sighed "We had better cancel it or I will never hear the last of it"

"I will set the wheels in motion to cancel your agreement and return your deposit to you in full. I should warn you that it takes a while to grind its way through the system but I can see that we have your bank details already, so that will speed things up."

Once Mickey got hold of it Sharon had a feeling that the Kentons were unlikely to see a penny of their money.

Reichenbach

Mickey eased the Jag down the country lanes. No need for speed. Just sit back and enjoy the ride. Away from the city, there seemed to be so much more room. He counted the whole corridor between London and the sea as the city. After all, they called Brighton London-on-Sea and there were developments all the way down the A23.

Away into the south downs though, the sky seemed to open up and houses were few and far between. Over the crest of a hill, he caught a glimpse of the house. It was old, nothing flashy, just solid, substantial bricks and mortar and land, acres and acres of land.

The call had been quite specific. "An appointment has been arranged for you with Derek Sanderson at Sutton House on Wednesday at one-thirty. You will receive an invitation in the post. Please be punctual."

There had been no opportunity to decline or reschedule. No discussion about convenience. Just an instruction. Money talks, thought Mickey.

As he approached the impressive entrance gates they swung open soundlessly. Either someone was very trusting or he was being watched. The gravel driveway wound off and over the hill, flanked on one side by a well-manicured beech hedge on the other by a run of Lombardy poplars.

The more Mickey looked, the more perfect it became – hedges had been trimmed, grass cut, fences painted – weeds dare not show their faces here he thought. A place like this just shouted out that its owner had made it.

Normally, the F-type was the stand-out car in any car park but here there was serious competition. As the driveway approached the house Mickey found himself behind a Ferrari Boxster and a Bentley.

He watched as a face he recognised in a white jacket checked the credentials of the Bentley driver and directed him to the front of the house.

The driver of the Ferrari climbed out and handed over his keys. White jacket beckoned over a driver to park the car. Mickey pulled forward as the Boxster sped off.

"Could I have your name please sir" white jacket was on autopilot

"Hello Brian." said Mickey "You are looking very smart".

White jacket looked up from his list "Mickey Fisher as I live and breathe. Last time I saw you was in the remand centre. We was both going to go straight as I recall."

"And I have" Mickey smiled "As a die"

"I would love to believe you, but your presence here in a flashy motor tells me a different story. You need to get out by the way. It's valet parking here today."

Mickey turned off the engine and climbed out. "You let the Bentley through"

"That is on account of it containing the Chairman and him having his own driver. I tell you, Mickey, I don't know what brings you here, but I have never seen so much wedge assembled in one place at one time.

Most of them are rolling in it and those that aren't - want to be. There is everyone here Judges, MP's, Policemen the lot. There is temptation all around. You need to watch your step."

Close to, the house was much grander than it looked with a range of outbuildings set to either side of the main building. As Mickey walked up to the front door, he noticed a small girl riding a pony in a paddock away to the left of what were, presumably, stables. A young blonde woman wearing a riding helmet was watching her whilst talking on the phone.

Attached to the front door was a large printed sign: *Reichenbach garden party this way.*

As he entered the central hall he could see through a set of double doors into the garden. The Ferrari driver was on the terrace with a group of middle-aged, well-heeled men. They all seemed easy in each other's company.

A waiter offered him champagne. Mickey declined. He needed to keep his wits about him today of all days. An effortlessly elegant Asian girl in a black dress appeared by his side.

"Mister Fisher?" Mickey nodded taking in her slim, body and long legs. "Derek is waiting for you in his office. Please go through". She directed Mickey into a panelled study clad in limed oak.

Derek Sanderson was sitting behind a large desk looking for all the world like a bank manager on dress down Friday.

"Mister Fisher. Good morning. Sanderson. Call me Derek. It is always nice to put a face to a name and you come well recommended." He rose to shake Mickey's hand perfunctorily. He had a way about him that discouraged disagreement.

Mickey perched on one of the large burgundy coloured leather chairs.

"Drink? Tea? Coffee? Something stronger?"

"I am fine thanks" said Mickey. "Nice house".

"Yes. Comfortable, well proportioned and ideally located. Forgive me - I sound like an estate agent."

Mickey looked around the room. Understated elegance seemed to describe it although on the wall was a picture of Sanderson shaking hands with...

"Is that who I think it is?"

"It is always a good idea to show off any contact with the royals don't you think?"

"Very nice."

"The house is Georgian originally but a previous owner knocked all the character out of it in the seventies so that he could keep an eye on his racehorses without having to get up too early."

"I saw some horses on the way in".

"They are just working ponies. This was a Sheik with a stable full of thoroughbreds. He converted an entire floor upstairs into a suite just so he could lay in bed and admire the view. The problem was it was all listed.

The conversion caused a bit of trouble locally but with the liberal application of petrodollars, all that seemed to go away. Unfortunately, he was unable to complete on a deal that went bad and it dropped into my lap for a song."

Mickey could imagine the consequences of failing to complete a deal with Derek Sanderson. The Sheik had got off lightly.

"I would give you the guided tour but I am a bit busy today as you can see. I have an investment committee meeting this afternoon and I need an update from you about the little project you are managing for the fund."

"So far so good." Mickey shifted in his seat. He realised that he was facing the sun. "We are carrying on presenting to potential customers. Too soon to say whether we have any takers yet from yesterday's bunch but I am confident from the way the presentation went that we should pick up fifty per cent of them – about five hundred in cash terms."

"Nice start" Sanderson tinkered with the keyboard of his computer. "It would be nice to get ten million from the initial stage and we are a quarter of the way there.

That might not seem much for a residential investment of this scale but Phase two will add a zero or two to that.

Any problems I should know about? Money? Staffing?"

Mickey smiled "Kevin is a bit of a find. He had them eating out of his hand"

Sanderson nodded approvingly "He always does. I have known him ever since his days as a currency trader. He never fails."

"There was a potential problem early yesterday afternoon but it was dealt with it quickly."

Sanderson peered at Mickey over the computer screen. "Problem? What sort of problem?"

"Oh, it was nothing. One of the couples had a Spanish lawyer as a son-in-law"

"Ah...best avoided."

Mickey nodded

"Any other problems I should know about?"

Mickey shook his head. "Nothing I can't handle"

"I am extremely glad to hear it. We won't be meeting again. As I am sure you are aware we are a hands-off investor and we prefer to keep contact to a minimum. We don't want anyone getting the wrong idea."

"How long have we got?"

"As soon as the account shows you have met the target locally, we will move the operation over to Spain then Phase two can begin. Any other questions?"

"What is this garden party? What is Reichenbach?"

"The Reichenbach falls are where Sherlock Holmes met his end. I gather it was a name drawn out of a hat by a previous chairman.

This is all about corporate marketing Mister Fisher. As well as the main investors these are all the people that make things happen. They are all important members of their communities – the councils; the lodges; the police. They set the framework in which a fund like ours thrives but we have to give a bit back to the community. In this case a garden party.

They will drink our wine and eat our food and go away armed with our fund report - all the while satisfying themselves that we are a good vehicle to invest in."

"They have no idea?"

"That they are investing in criminality? Nothing is further from their minds. RF is one of the top-performing fund managers. All of our funds are top quartile. Mostly we invest in things that they recognise - shares, government bonds, real estate – things like that.

Projects like this are buried under alternatives and take a ridiculously small proportion of the money in play so they never get around to reading about that as long as the returns keep rolling in.

Investment management is all about trust. Our clients trust us to invest their money to their best advantage. This project has been evaluated and a risk profile created for it. The profiling assumes that a small proportion of investments go bad and we balance our risk exposure accordingly."

Sanderson rose to indicate the meeting was over.

"I need to go and play the good host. Hang around and have a drink and a bite to eat. Mingle. According to my wife, the tapas are particularly good."

The two men moved into the hallway. Sanderson paused "We only have a limited window to complete phase one. By limited I mean weeks. It won't take long for some nosy reporter to start looking into Estados and we don't want that kind of attention. Be ready to shut down the Brighton office and move everything to Torremolinos in a couple of weeks."

Derek Sanderson swept off to mix with his guests leaving Mickey in the hall.

"Champagne?" offered the waiter again. This time Mickey took a glass from the tray and wandered out onto the terrace. He could do with a drink and something to eat but he felt uncomfortable.

The great and the good of county society were not his cup of tea at all. He had spotted a half-decent pub on the main road that looked far more his style.

"You look lost"

Mickey smiled at the Asian woman who had greeted him. Her long, straight, black hair offsetting her black dress and adding to her attractiveness. "Not lost, just dipping my toes into the water."

"Derek asked me to look after you and make sure that you don't get eaten. There are more sharks in these waters than you would think."

"Are you Mrs Sanderson? He said...."

"No, she is away. I am his PA that he likes to show off at events like this. My name is Jasmine. I take it you don't know anyone here?"

Mickey shook his head

"It is quite the guest list. Over there in the tweed jacket is Jackman, a junior minister in the last Government, in conversation with the current leader of the County Council. Talking to the chairman of United Insurance in the blazer is Hugo Proudfoot, Deputy Chief Constable. Just by the shrubbery..."

"I understand" Mickey interrupted "I am way out of my depth here. I think it best if I slip away before any of them notice me."

"There is no need to run away so soon. I hate it every bit as much as you do and I won't have anyone to talk to."

Mickey took a sip of the champagne "Investment isn't your subject then?"

She smiled "Not really. I have no illusions as to why I am here. Derek doesn't want to say that he is the alpha male, he just lets the guests know by showing them. I am part of that fantasy."

"Some fantasy"

"It is a better living than hustling in the West End which is where he found me. Are you married, Mickey? Courting?"

Mickey nodded. Jasmine tossed her head like one of the Sheik's thoroughbred mares.

"A shame. Sex is the common currency here whether Derek is showing it off, having it or offering it to others."

The thought of sex with Derek Sanderson's personal assistant filled Mickey with desire - then excitement. "Perhaps we could meet up for a drink" he muttered.

Mickey was used to chancing his arm with women. He had read somewhere that Casanova was not particularly handsome or rich – he seduced as many women as he did because he asked. Mickey took the view that it didn't matter if he was knocked back – at least he had tried.

To his surprise Jasmine pouted. "That would be nice. Perhaps somewhere more conducive." She pressed a card into his hand. "Give me a ring." She waved him goodbye and moved on across the terrace.

* * *

"Short visit" observed Brian as he waited for his car. "Too rich for your blood?"

Mickey grimaced "Just a bit of business. That's all."

"Have you made sure you've still got all your fingers?" He handed Mickey his keys "Be good" he said, "and if you can't be good..."

"Be careful"

Mickey smiled as the Jag accelerated off down the driveway. Risk profiling. He would use that argument to placate Sharon.

From the terrace Jasmine watched him go. She caught Sanderson's eye. "Contact made?" he asked.

"Yes," she smiled "He is a poor frightened little puppy at the moment – but he won't be able to resist."

"Keep him close" said Sanderson.

Analysis

The villa was well positioned on the outskirts of the city and had the benefit of being in a development of identical buildings and therefore anonymous. The landlord had been only too keen to let it for six months to the Government at top dollar. He had even left them a basket of fruit as a welcome present. The four-bedrooms were all spacious and the kitchen was doubling as a makeshift office.

The gallery of photographs were spread across the table – cataloguing the previous evening's activities. Rojo was studying one of the groups with a small magnifying glass. Although in truth, they had not achieved very much, the photographs gave the investigation substance and focus.

These men were up to something he felt sure. What turned it from a dinner amongst colleagues into a conspiracy was the presence of the fourth man. That and the whispers about the abuse of power and crooked deals involving Mijas. What they were conspiring about was the key question and Rojo was no nearer knowing the answer.

He stood and stretched "So, inspectors, what do we know?"

Baltasar shrugged his shoulders "What we think we know and what we can prove are different things. We think we know that Mijas is using his position to sell building permits for new apartments. We have conversations but, as yet no testimony.

We think that Parador, his head of planning, is also in it up to his neck. We can tie him to this latest development – the one they call Aguilera - but that is in the public domain. They are using Judge Diamante to provide legal cover if they are challenged. We don't know who the fourth man at the dinner was but the word was that they were meeting the money man that evening."

"And we think he is English" Toro often felt a little intimidated in these open debates and was delighted when Rojo nodded and smiled.

"Indeed we do. Have we checked our database of ex-pats?"

Toro nodded "Nothing shows up. His photo isn't known to us but maybe our friends in the UK can help. So far we don't have a name."

"What about the two you picked up after the restaurant?"

"We kept them overnight and we'll have to let them go this morning. I see little point in arresting them for assaulting the journalist unless he wants to prefer charges himself."

"Did we learn anything from them?"

"Almost nothing. According to them, they are just drivers that Mijas uses from time to time to ferry people around. When we searched them we did find an access card in the name of Scott MacDonald and a parking ticket for the multi-storey at Malaga airport. Huertas, the shorter one, was parked there from 8:55 yesterday for two hours. He admits he was collecting someone but claims that he never knew his name."

Rojo banged the bed with the flat of his hand. "So, this is something we know. Good work Toro. Let's find out who he was picking up. That will give us a name to work with."

"We should ask him again." Baltasar was well aware that Toro was a useful persuader of recalcitrant criminals "Less politely this time. How did he know who to pick up without a name? Maybe the CCTV at the airport will help."

"Perhaps he knew him by sight" Rojo was looking at the group picture again with his glass "Maybe this isn't the first time the Englishman has graced our country."

Baltasar picked up his phone "I will send Rio down to the airport to check the CCTV and go through the passenger lists."

"Start with the flights from the UK within that two-hour window. I will talk to Madrid. Toro, have another chat with our guests and see if you can elicit a name."

"That will take time to arrange." Toro pulled a face. "The locals are a bit precious about giving us access. They hate it that the CNP is hassling them over what they see as a local matter. While I am waiting, I will go to the airport with Rio to stop her from getting into any trouble."

"You should be careful she doesn't get you into trouble" Rojo smiled.

They watched the departing bulk of Toro as he left the room. "Madrid?" Baltasar's eyebrows were raised

"If I need to talk to London – first I need to talk to Madrid. You know how it works"

"I know that the fewer people that hear about this the better – especially in Madrid"

"I won't broadcast it. I'll talk to the Council President and tell him it is sensitive - that way we keep them onside. We don't want Hector Diamante hearing on the grapevine that we are focusing on him."

"Who is Scott MacDonald? The name seems familiar"

"Wasn't there a footballer called MacDonald?" Rojo was scratching his head "I don't follow it but I remember something about his knee and him having to retire."

"You are right. He played for Malaga I think. Why should one of Mijas' heavies have his access card?"

"Perhaps we should find out. Do we know where it gives access to?"

"No clue. What about the journalist? Do you think he knows anything?"

Rojo grimaced "I am sure he does but like all journalists, there will be a gap between rumour and fact. I don't doubt that we will be able to have an interesting conversation, but I doubt that it will uncover any hard evidence."

"I will send Rio down to the hospital to have a sniff around. I think we need to keep her here as boots on the ground."

"All I sense so far is smoke and mirrors. This is someone who is used to disguising his real intentions. Do you think the CNI would have an interest in him?"

"I can always ask but you know what the spooks are like – even if they do know something they might not tell us."

* * *

The two detectives had been waiting for some time. Their request for information contravened several regulations to do with privacy and access and had, therefore, to be referred up for sanction. Similarly, access to CCTV footage required approval from the airport management.

Rio passed the time watching as each flight disgorged its passengers into the terminal. Unruly children accompanying their dishevelled parents many of whom had partaken liberally of the alcohol provided as if a holiday provided the perfect excuse for overindulgence. "Most of them are families" she observed, "A single man should be easy to spot."

Toro was getting impatient. They had been at the airport for over an hour while their request was received, processed, passed to a higher authority and then delegated down to this girl on this terminal.

Why was everything so complicated? Toro was a policeman. In the old days he would have just taken out his identification and his gun and they would have complied immediately.

Rio smiled sweetly. "Flights WS1436 and AY230?"

The girl on the terminal sighed "I will print them out for you but there are over two hundred names on those lists."

"Just English. Print out just the English ones" He instructed.

The girl sighed again. "It's not that easy. I will print them all out with their nationality and passport details then you can cross out the ones you don't want"

It was Toro's turn to sigh but before he could respond Rio touched him lightly on the arm. "That will be splendid," She said and smiled again. The girl was rather pretty.

* * *

"If we assume that we are right in our assumptions, we should be able to find a money trail linking all four suspects." Baltasar pinned Mijas picture in the centre of the board propped up on the dressing table. "We need to have a look at their bank accounts and see if our friends at the tax office have any information that might help."

Rojo nodded in agreement "I will arrange the orders. If they have any sense we are looking for offshore accounts in protected locations."

Baltasar shrugged "Maybe for Mijas or Diamante but Parador is a local, small-town guy who probably needs access to the cash. He will have it stashed where he can get at it easily."

"So we should look at the closest options: Gibraltar; the Channel Islands; maybe Switzerland first of all."

"My money is on Gibraltar. It is only a couple of hours away by car. No costly, inconvenient flights needed and plenty of opportunities to launder any cash using the local casinos."

Rojo nodded "I agree. Let's see what we can uncover. Parador seems to be the weakest link but we will still need to interview Judge Diamante. Knowing him, I would not be surprised if he would dump the others in the face of a decent deal that would allow him to retire without losing face. I doubt that the others have anything on him."

"He cannot need the money – unless he has very expensive vices"

"He certainly lives well but his Achilles heel is his vanity, not his money. I have met him many times at legal functions. He is breathtakingly arrogant and always needs to be the expert in the room. Part of him will welcome an interview – it would make him the centre of our attention."

The third picture was pinned to the board above the other two. "What about Mijas?" Baltasar shrugged "My instinct is that if we go after him openly, he will do a bunk and I don't fancy years of trying to get him back from Morocco or wherever else he ends up."

"Again, I detect arrogance. He expects us to interview him. He has managed to see off investigations before – what makes this any different?"

Baltasar was keen to return to their office in the Salamanca district. "Apart from the interviews, I think we would be better off back at base for the next phase of the investigation. I will set up the key one with the Mayor as a priority, as for Parador my instinct is to let him sweat. We can talk to him when we are clear what the others are saying"

* * *

They sat in the departures lounge going through the long list of passengers. Toro watched from the bar as a steady stream of people trudged in and out of the space. For most this was the end of their holidays. Generally, they looked exhausted, hungover and out of sorts. The airport facilities provided them with a final sting to make their day complete.

"Twenty euros," said the barman. Toro was stunned "Excuse me. Could you repeat that?"

"Two coffees at ten euros each" the barman was well used to outrage. It was no wonder the passengers looked miserable, thought Toro, as he passed over a twenty euro note. "I only wanted two coffees, not the whole café" he muttered as he carried the tray back to their table.

Rio was engrossed in the task. Too much policing was carried out on computers these days she thought. This was good, old fashioned data analysis using a listing and a red pen.

"What about Americans? Or Irish? We have both on here."

"Did you think our man looked like an American?"

"No. Too smart and the Irish guy is with his family"

Once the families had been discounted and the British identified there seemed to be only one possibility. She passed it over to Toro, still seething over the price of the coffee.

"It is not as if it is anything special. It comes out of a machine."

"Derek Sanderson is the only one," she said, "Do we know anything about a Derek Sanderson?"

Toro examined the analysis closely "Unless he was travelling with someone else and went to the dinner alone" he said. "Let's see what Baltasar thinks."

"Back to see that pretty stewardess I think," said Rio "We need to check the CCTV to identify Mr Sanderson as the right man."

Brighton

Detective Inspector J Buckland. The nameplate laid claim to the office. Butler opened the office door with trepidation. He never liked taking over existing teams. Like most policemen, despite all the talk of common standards and conformity, he had his way of doing things and liked to build his own team. It was particularly bad in this case because of the sudden death of Buckland.

DI Jack Buckland had been a career officer. For nearly twenty-five years he had been a Detective Sergeant in the Met - latterly in the Fraud Squad. Then he bought himself a new, young wife and, in need of the money, took and passed his Inspectors exams – moving to the Sussex force shortly afterwards. Whether it was the stress of the job, the demands of his new Thai bride or years of abusing his heart and lungs with alcohol and cigarettes was not clear. However, at around 10 pm one Wednesday evening he passed out at his desk and wasn't found until the next morning - by which time he was long dead.

"This was where it happened" Butler started - he had not heard Davies arrive. "We cleared the place up a bit, took out all the governor's stuff and so on"

Butler surveyed the desk gloomily, cleared of everything except a large, untidy heap of files. Although his office in London had been impersonal at least it was a decent size. This was a broom cupboard by comparison. "Bad karma" he muttered.

"Dead man's shoes you mean?" Davies shared his misgivings. "The problem is we don't have anywhere else for you to go. Space is a bit cramped around here."

"I am sure it will be fine once I have opened the window and smartened it up a bit."

Davies pointed to the files. "This is all the stuff in progress at the time of.... Well all the stuff the boss was working on anyway"

He shuffled back to the doorway, uneasy at his own insensitivity. "I'll be down the hall if you need me."

"I seem to be missing a computer."

Davies shrugged

"The Governor didn't like them so he had it taken away. The only thing he would ever use was the fax."

He indicated the cream coloured machine in the corner.

"Fax machine? These went out with the Ark. I thought it was a printer."

Davies shrugged. "Apparently email is too expensive or too insecure or something. God doesn't like it either so we still use fax"

"How do you keep in contact with say, the Spanish police?"

Davies suspected a trap. "When you say keep in contact with...what do you mean exactly?"

"Well. I had assumed that liaison involved a bit of liaising on a regular basis and that that would involve contact between say my opposite number in Madrid and me – for example. If I don't have an email address how will he or she get in touch with me? By phone? Carrier pigeon?"

Davies shrugged again "They don't ring up – as far as I know. If they want us to see something they send a fax"

"Welcome to the 21st century" Butler hadn't imagined that a move to Sussex would also be a step backwards in time. "I'll talk to Smallbone."

Butler moved the chair away from the desk and sat down gingerly.

What seemed like moments later Davies appeared at the door with a mug. "Tea skipper"

Butler looked up. He had ploughed his way through half the buff folders on his desk.

"Two sugars?"

Davies nodded "You have been busy"

"Mostly thieving. Small scale stuff. I have been trying to make connections to see if we have just a few bad boys or whether everyone is at it."

"Best to assume they are all villains I find" Davies grinned broadly "By the by Proudfoot wants to see you. Sometime this morning he said"

"As in ACC Proudfoot – also known as the hand of God, or just God for short."

"The very same. He has an office on the third floor"

* * *

"Enter" The office was large, too large for the one desk occupying it. It is no wonder they are short of space Butler mused to himself. A tall man with grey hair was sitting at the desk. A pair of rimless spectacles gave him an almost sinister appearance. By his side, peering over his shoulder was a small,

67

squat woman wearing the full uniform of a Superintendent of Police.

"DI Butler. Hugo Proudfoot. Welcome to the Division" Butler shook the extended hands. "This is Amanda Smallbone." A limp, almost deferential, handshake from her and a glimpse of a smile. " I hope they are looking after you"

Butler nodded appreciatively. They seemed friendly enough.

"I know that you are likely to be very busy - picking up speed and so on - but I thought it was important to make myself known to you.

As you know, the circumstances of your appointment are particularly unfortunate. Jack Buckland was a well-liked and well-respected officer. In many ways, he will be a hard act to follow.

I have been reading your file and I am sure that a detective of your experience and seniority is just what is required. So I welcome that and look forward to working with you."

Butler smiled and waited for the ifs and buts

"We are under no little pressure in this Division on both results and costs. Our political masters seem intent on expecting the earth from the former whilst they have a firm hold on our testicles over the latter. This has some implications for how we operate strategically and tactically.

You might have noticed that we have a very lean structure here. Operational control is vested in me. Not only is Superintendent Smallbone my deputy but she has full line responsibility and acts in my name in respect of interventions – tactical firearms and so on. We have no DCIs in post. You report directly to me alongside the other DIs who you will meet around the place."

"This is, of course, an opportunity to run your team free from overt interference from above and it means that I trust you to do so unless you give me a reason to have doubts. I will manage based on the two pillars of results and costs. Amanda?"

Butler visualised the large expense claim sitting on his desk

"The downside of a lean structure is that we have to spread special responsibilities across the division." Smallbone was here to deliver the bad news. "Specifically Jack Buckland was responsible for liaison with our colleagues in the rest of the UK and overseas. It has to be said that this is not particularly onerous. It involves a couple of meetings in London a year and occasionally looking after officers visiting from other climes. Apart from that, we get regular stuff from organisations like Europol that needs digesting".

Proudfoot snorted contemptuously. "Binning would be more apt. Shall we say some of these foreign police forces are more interested in the amount of gold braid on their uniform than good policing." The irony was lost on him. "Frankly we have more than enough to do looking after the criminals that live in the Home Counties without pursuing those that have escaped to Spain - however ill-gotten their gains."

Butler raised an eyebrow "Is illegal importation an issue? We appear to manage quite a long bit of coastline"

Proudfoot sat back in his chain, deferring to Smallbone. "From a liaison standpoint certainly. The Border Force is certainly one of the stakeholders but generally, they like to manage their own operations.

Similarly the intelligence services and counter-terrorism."

"The problem is that all these things consume resources" Proudfoot was engaged again "I don't see how I am expected to ensure the lives of the residents of Sussex go by relatively crime-free whilst also having to keep an eye on all the whackos and fundamentalists of whatever persuasion that visit the country legally or otherwise. Certainly not from my budget."

Proudfoot stood up abruptly. It was clear the interview was over.

"Look. I have to go to another meeting. Amanda, will you escort DI Butler back to the first floor. I am sure you have plenty to discuss." He shook Butler's hand again "Good luck. I am counting on you"

* * *

Smallbone closed the office door behind them. "Interesting approach" ventured Butler, quietly.

"But effective, in a limited way" Smallbone led the way down the corridor "You run your own team until there is a cock up and then there is hell to pay"

"He seems reasonably humane" smiled Butler

"Not from him – from me. Don't listen to all that bollocks about operational control. I run the division. Proudfoot goes to the cocktail parties and hobnobs with the Chief Constable. If you need anything – come to me. If I need anything from you I will let you know."

"I take it that he doesn't know"

"About your real reason for being here? No. Nor does he need to."

"So as far as the NCA are concerned, you are the main contact."

70

"The only contact. The fewer people in this particular loop, the better."

They paused outside Butler's door. The plate with Buckland's name on it had been unscrewed and dropped in the waste bin inside the doorway.

"Things move on" muttered Butler. Smallbone sighed. "Despite the roll of honour reeled off for your benefit just now Jack Buckland was a dinosaur. Very clubbable. Always first to the bar but a short-sighted, narrow-minded dinosaur, nevertheless. He saw liaison as a perk – an opportunity to jolly at the forces expense - whereas it is an essential part of catching criminals. Open borders, whether real or imagined, make it easier for them – but also easier for us."

"At the NCA we are dealing with people that operate on a global scale."

"and that has implications for how we police this area" Smallbone smiled that half-smile again "We can't afford to set borders on our ability to operate.

I too have read your file and I can see that you are wasted here. In addition to opening the door to international co-operation as was requested, the liaison job so underplayed by Proudfoot is a treasure chest of quick wins.

By now, good old Sergeant Davies will have offloaded all the crap in the system onto your desk. Hoping that you will bury yourself in every two-bit burglary that they haven't had the time or inclination to deal with properly and leave him alone to cherry-pick the jobs that will support his attempts to climb the greasy pole to DI."

"My advice to you is to delegate it back to him. The reason I allocated Davies to you is that he has an encyclopaedic knowledge of all the instances of criminality that have stained our portals over the past twenty years. Whereas legislation may require that, officially, we have to forget, it doesn't require Sergeant Davies to do so."

Butler nodded. "Thanks for that. I don't appear to have a laptop by the way."

Smallbone hesitated "I assumed that you would be bringing one with you. It is a secondment after all. I will arrange one with all the necessary permissions."

"While you are here could you oblige me with a signature"

Smallbone cast her eye over the expense claim and bunch of receipts stapled to it. She signed it at the bottom

"My other advice is not to take the piss concerning expenses. I don't know how much of this is genuine and I don't want to know. Just remember that when it comes to spoofs – I wrote the rulebook."

That half-smile again

"Received and understood" She shut the door behind her as she left.

Butler surveyed the two piles of files. Was it his imagination or had the "to read" pile increased in size while he had been upstairs? He opened the door again

"Sergeant Davies" he yelled.

Hospital

Rio flashed her ID card to the uniformed officer on the door. Following the beating, Rojo had insisted on a police guard at the hospital to protect him as he could be an important witness. Grudgingly, the local force had agreed to provide protection.

Matthews was plugged into various machines monitoring different bodily functions. A drip was attached to his left arm. An attractive nurse was checking a clipboard attached to his bed.

Her dark eyes sparkled as Rio approached taking in all the aspects of her body on display.

"How is my boy doing?"

The nurse smiled. "You are his mother?" Rio was affronted but put on her sweetest and, in her view, her most seductive smile. The nurse's eyes responded, "No. I see you are much too young."

"He is in my charge"

"You are police then?"

She looked through the notes. As well as broken ribs, the doctors had uncovered a ruptured spleen, numerous abrasions, a broken nose and a dislocated collar bone. It all looked pretty painful.

Matthews woke with a start. "I need to ask Mijas some questions about Aguilera."

Rio smiled again. What she liked about this Englishman was that he never knew when to give up. Despite his beating, he was still determined to carry on. The nurse was less impressed.

"I doubt that you will be able to do so for some time. You have lost quite a lot of blood."

Matthews turned his head towards Rio.

"Who are you?"

"I am here to protect you and, perhaps, find out what you know about Senor Mijas already."

The nurse's defences sprang into action. "This patient is not well enough to answer any questions"

Rio backed off immediately. "Of course not. Nothing he says in this state would be admissible as evidence anyway. We will wait until he is ready for a formal interview."

The nurse relaxed again. "It is just that the doctor's instructions...."

"Of course. It is not a problem. I will just wait here until my colleague comes to relieve me."

Mollified, the nurse turned to leave.

"What time does your shift end? Perhaps we could have a drink later..."

Slowly, the nurse turned back to Rio. "We could – but I am not sure my husband would approve" and with another flash of those eyes, she was gone.

"Lucky guy" Rio murmured "Now, Senor Matthews, tell me, what is Aguilera?"

Matthews licked his lips, unsure of his bargaining position. "I need some guarantees" he croaked

"You heard what I said to your nurse?" Matthews nodded "It was true. We couldn't rely on anything that you said in this condition. You are not a suspect in our investigation but we could use your help.

You have been studying Mayor Mijas for some time I guess and from what we know already whatever it is that is going on has been happening for all that time."

"For as long as we have been running the Enquirer."

"Personally I will make sure that when we arrest these bastards, you will be first to know.

Will that do as a guarantee?"

Matthews groaned as he reached for the glass of water. Rio held it to his mouth so that he could use the straw. "We can also prosecute the two hoodlums who did this to you if that is what you want."

Matthews began softly "Aguilera is a development of two hundred luxury villas and apartments just off the A45 inside the boundary of the national park."

Rio raised an eyebrow "I thought national parks were protected from development?"

"They are except in cases of exceptional economic need. No prizes for guessing who decides that a need is exceptional enough."

"The Mayor presumably"

Matthews attempted to nod and grimaced in pain. "This is not the first time he has declared such a need – but it is one of the most blatant. To attract the foreigners he has allowed the scheme to be expanded to include elements of retail and leisure, making it a full-blown commercial centre."

"But the region will benefit economically right?"

"Probably, but the main beneficiaries will be the development company involved and, I believe, the Mayor himself. Remember that this is all at the expense of a special environmental habitat."

"You think he is taking kickbacks? Do you have any evidence?"

"Until recently we have had lots of rumours and people only prepared to comment off the record. Now we have something harder anyway, I rather thought it was you who should be gathering evidence, not me."

Rio smiled again "Touché"

"It is not just him. There are others involved. Whether they are paid off or not I don't know but it is amazing that anyone in a position to challenge his authority has been remarkably silent."

"Have you done any digging? About Mijas and the kickbacks in particular"

"We are a small regional newspaper. We don't have the resources to investigate financial behaviour. We are close to the ground. We have eyes and ears locally but nothing else.

I tried to get one of the nationals involved but Mijas got wind of it and they dropped their interest under threat of a lawsuit and advised us to do the same."

Rio was making notes "Interesting. Do you have any corroboration?"

"No. I was just told that the editor had lunch with Judge Diamante and canned the feature when he returned to the office."

"Even more interesting. It is funny how the same old names keep cropping up isn't it?"

Matthews looked at her quizzically "Jesus" he said "It goes that far up. I had assumed that it stopped with Mijas."

Rio shook her head "I am saying nothing and, if I were you, I would make sure I had concrete evidence before trying to expose someone as embedded in the establishment as Judge Diamante."

Matthews pressed the bell for the nurse. "I need to get out of here," he said, "I have a newspaper to run."

The nurse with the dark eyes hurried into the room looking flustered followed by a doctor.

"I thought my instructions were clear - no visitors and no questions. Please leave." The doctor gesticulated at the door.

Rio stood slowly "We have to keep him safe, anyway we were just chatting," she said "At Mister Matthew's request.

No harm done."

The doctor stood back to let her pass "I will be the judge of that."

Rio smiled at the nurse who was doing her best to hide behind the doctor.

"Talk to Scottie if you want the truth," said Matthews as she strolled out of the door.

* * *

The office was big, but not palatially so, with a view across the lush green park. Rojo could see people taking advantage of the shade provided by the palm trees to just stroll along the dusty paths.

Generally, the tone of the room was modest – befitting an elected representative of the people. On the walls were a couple of pictures of the Mayor shaking hands with famous visitors. He recognised Bill Clinton, the other was an actor. He knew the face but couldn't recall the name.

"Banderas," said Baltasar "He comes from around here." Rojo nodded in recognition.

A secretary bustled in with some papers and placed them on the large desk.

"The Mayor will be with you shortly. Help yourself to water" She indicated the cooler in the corner as she hurried out as if not wanting to be contaminated by their presence.

"I see we merit the best china," said Baltasar, contemplating a paper cone of chilled water.

"No doubt that is reserved for those they are trying to impress." Rojo was becoming bored. "I am pretty sure that they don't have to wait either."

"Stupid power games" Baltasar stood and stretched "A little bit more evidence and I would handcuff him in front of his staff and march him out of the building."

"Sorry to keep you waiting Gentlemen." If Mijas had heard he gave no sign of it. "I was at siesta. I was sorry to hear that the custom has all but faded away in Madrid but it is the way we do things down here."

Rojo shook his hand "Jesus Rojo. Thank you for seeing us at such short notice. Our time in Malaga is limited as you know."

"If I can be of assistance I am happy to do so. We seldom get national bodies asking for our opinions on policy. We are usually receivers, not contributors."

Rojo smiled "We value all contributions from wherever they may come but we are anxious to pick your brains in areas where you have considerable experience particularly regional development."

Mijas sat back in his chair and raised his arms expansively. "Then you have come to the right man. Let me give you some background." He pressed a button on his desk and a screen unfurled soundlessly from the ceiling showing slides of the region.

"What you see around us here is the city only. This is of course my primary responsibility but when it comes to regional development you have to think wider. Malaga the city has around six hundred thousand inhabitants.

Malaga the region has over one and a half million. All these people need jobs and security. We have the port, of course, and agriculture but we are dependent upon one industry – tourism.

Our strategy is to develop opportunities to broaden the economy into other areas like manufacturing, retail and leisure and to build the stock of disposable income so that..."[1]

Rojo held up his hand to stop the lecture. "Mister Mayor. I am sure this impresses local businessmen but, as I am sure you are aware, we are more interested in specific projects."

For the briefest of seconds Mijas' eyes narrowed. "Naturally," he said amiably "Which projects would you like to know about?"

Baltasar was bored with the pretence. "We are looking at all the development projects that required special permission over the past five years."

Mijas raised an eyebrow "That could be quite a few. I am not sure how many"

"In particular we are interested in the development known as Aguilera" Rojo intervened.

He smiled grimly "and you have heard the whispers that the process was corrupt and that I have been pocketing vast sums for signing permissions."

"Not for the first time," said Baltasar.

"It is, I am sad to say, part of being a public figure" Mijas shrugged "I have been active in local and regional politics for twenty years. I have learned that you seldom get credit for the good things that you do but, for sure, you will always get knocked for making the difficult decisions."

Baltasar cleared his throat "and you are not compensated at all for taking these difficult decisions despite the rumours?"

"My finances are a matter of public record. Yes, I am a wealthy man. I was lucky to come from a wealthy family. My hotels provide me with an annuity income. I donate my salary as Mayor to charity.

I do not need to be compensated for making the right decisions for the city and the region."

Rojo had a flashback to the peace of the valley being disturbed by chainsaws.

"Some might argue that in this case, you are flouting the legislation that established the protection of an unique habitat."

"Environmental protection is important but so is economic development. Despite the efforts of Madrid, this region is almost entirely dependent upon tourism. If some calamity were to befall that industry, the livelihoods of the majority of the people would be at risk.

As Mayor, I have to balance environmental protection against the development of a more balanced economy every day.

That is what I mean by taking difficult decisions. Of course, it would be ideal if Aguilera were outside the park boundary but in fact, it takes under one per cent of the park area and will deliver a significant number of jobs.

I judge that to be worthwhile – I don't need to be persuaded by bribes whatever the rumours say."

"We understand that there may be foreign money involved in..." Baltasar began.

"Are these more rumours?" snapped Mijas "No doubt you have been talking to that gringo Matthews and his cheap little rag. I swear that if he publishes any more lies about this I will sue his miserable arse until he is down to his last euro."

"Your men were a little more direct than that the other evening." Rojo leaned back in his chair enjoying Baltasar's ability to get under a suspect's skin. "Mister Matthews is in hospital with multiple injuries as a result"

"Yes. They can be a little over-enthusiastic when they come across people sticking their noses where they are not required."

Mijas drew himself up to his full height, then, just as quickly, regained his self-control. "Gentlemen, you will have to excuse me. I have to attend a funeral at four. If you have any further questions I will do my best to answer them."

Rojo stood "Until we meet again."

Salamanca

Rio was self-aware to the point that it had been raised by her therapist. She examined her appearance in the long mirror determining whether her current outfit was fit for purpose. The tight black jeans and black sneakers given colour by the emerald green shirt. It was definitely up to the job.

"Do you have to go this early?" Anya stretched languidly on the bed allowing the sheet to fall slightly exposing more naked flesh. "We could have some more fun..."

She took in the wild black hair, the hazel eyes, the pouting lips and the body. "I have a meeting in the old town."

"To do with the bad men I told you about?"

Rio smiled "Yes" She sat next to her on the bed. "Do you have to go back to work today?"

Anya sighed "I should. I need the money and they are expecting me"

Rio stroked her face "A pity but I need to pass on the story you gave me"

Anya pushed her hand away "I am starting to think that you only invited yourself to stay so that you could pump me for information."

Rio could see that a simple denial was not going to be enough "No. Partly. Haven't you had a good time?"

She moved closer to kiss those inviting lips and was startled by the blow that came instead. She caught the retreating hand and twisted it causing Anya to wince. "So," she said "you want something a little rougher?" pinning her down on the bed. Anya kissed her passionately as Rio eased off her jacket.

"What about your meeting?"

"I have a feeling I am going to be a little late," said Rio.

* * *

Rojo paced up and down the narrow office. "We think he is English so let's talk to the English" Sanderson's face had been enlarged and placed on the board.

"We requested clearance three days ago but we haven't heard back yet" The frustration in Baltasar's voice was apparent.

Rojo shrugged "Have we stressed how urgent this is?"

Baltasar nodded "Of course but when have they ever had a sense of urgency about anything"

"I think we have given them enough time. I am assuming that it is cleared. Do we know who to contact?"

"I have some contacts with the London police but..."

"But?"

"Well, he could come from anywhere. There are dozens of different police forces in England"

"Don't they talk to each other?" It was Baltasar's turn to shrug.

"I know some drug squad detectives that came to Marbella last year." Toro was eager to contribute. Rojo nodded.

"I don't want to go through Europol. It is too bureaucratic and besides, it would take too long. We can't afford to wait any longer for the Justice Department and they would probably just opt for Europol anyway. So Inspectors, let us put our contacts to work initially and see where that takes us."

* * *

"Hello" The heavily-accented voice piqued Butler's interest immediately. He had been leafing through the latest Europol bulletin looking at the assorted con men, drug dealers, and wife beaters that had gone missing across the continent.

"Hello. Mr Butler, it is Toro"

Butler pictured a tall muscular figure in a tracksuit holding up Benny Trentham by the scruff of his neck.

"Toro the bull?"

"Yes. Of course Toro the bull"

"Do you have any more drug dealers for me?"

"No. No. There are not many like Mr Trentham over here now ever since our little clear out"

It was one of the most successful busts Butler could remember. Trentham's entire network was rolled up in two days and Toro was at the heart of the action in Spain. It sent a message to the whole criminal ex-pat community that they were not out of reach of the Met and led to wholesale departures from the Costas of Spain to safer places.

"I have someone, we think his name is Derek Sanderson. I wondered if I email you his picture you could run him through your database."

"Certainly. What has he done?"

"We are not sure. All we know is that he is English and that he was meeting with some bad men. Do you know the name?"

Butler decided to play it cool. "The name doesn't ring any bells. I will need to look him up. Email me the picture and I will see what I can do. I take it this is an unofficial request?"

Toro chuckled "I thought that I would save you all the paperwork"

"What might he have done?"

"To be honest we don't know where he fits in but we are working a big corruption case and he had dinner with our main suspects."

"No smoke without fire eh." The first picture, taken from the airport CCTV showed a slim, balding, bespectacled man but was otherwise indistinct. The second showed the same man sitting at a restaurant table.

Without a doubt, it was the same man he had seen in the file Craddock had given him on money laundering.

"Toro," he said "I can confirm that it is indeed Derek Sanderson and that he is known to us. I can tell you he is a person of interest in a number of ongoing investigations."

Toro understood perfectly "What do you think he has done?"

"I don't know the full scale of it - but I will make enquiries and let you know what I find. I do know that I have seen his picture in a file on money laundering."

"Thank you, Sir"

"Thank you, Toro and good luck with the investigation."

* * *

Anya was in tears, sobbing into her shoulder. Rio prised herself out of her arms and began gathering her outfit from the floor around the bed.

"I will be in Malaga. You will be in Madrid. I might never see you again."

"Perhaps you will be able to come to Madrid when it is over." Rio did up the final button on her shirt and stroked Anya's naked arm. "Anyway, I will be in Malaga for a long while yet.

Remember, this case is based here. I will be here all the time. Don't worry."

This seemed to quell the tears for a while as Rio eased on her jeans and adjusted her make-up. The slap had left a red mark on her cheekbone.

"Will you be back before I go to the restaurant?"

"What time do you leave?"

"Five o'clock."

Rio looked at her watch. "Once I have had my meeting I will try and get back as soon as I can."

Anya climbed out of bed and clung to her. She kissed her gently this time.

"I must go. I will see you later."

As she left the bedroom she caught a glimpse of Anya's naked body in the mirror. Taking her to Madrid could be a real option, meanwhile she would be enjoying her stay in Malaga.

* * *

87

Baltasar shut the lid of his laptop and stretched back in the chair "I am nervous about this English connection, it doesn't make any sense."

Rojo was still pacing, his brain working overtime. "How doesn't it make sense?"

"As far as we know we have a local Mayor selling building permits to developers – a relatively local, relatively mundane crime. Serious enough to merit our attention on principle but still mundane. Why involve a third party? – let alone from a foreign country. He is a rich man. He has a big house on the lake. It makes no sense."

"It has to be about value." Rojo stopped in front of his desk. "If he were just taking a payment for the building permits I would agree with you but why take the risk for such a meagre reward? If we suppose that he is also taking a share of the end value of the development that he has allowed we are talking about much larger sums of money. Surely it follows that he will be in cahoots with the developers themselves."

"So we think our Englishman is a developer"

"Maybe. Or the money behind the developer perhaps."

* * *

Butler drew a blank with the system and Craddock's phone was going to voicemail. There were three Derek Sandersons. Two of them were dead and one was serving a long stretch in Wandsworth for a string of violent offences.

Davies was more forthcoming "You won't find anything on there," he said scornfully "It's all data protection and human rights. The real gen is up here" He tapped his forehead meaningfully.

"Now let me see. There was a Derek Sanderson logged as a person of interest in a currency fraud case a couple of years ago. We felt his collar but we had to lay off him before he gave up anything. He is certainly a face. Looks like a bank manager."

Butler showed him the email

"That's the bloke. Bent as a corkscrew but very clever and very rich. Dangerous I would say. We had to drop him as a suspect because he is rumoured to be best mates with Proudfoot. We interview him. One phone call later and he is gone."

"How was he?"

"Urbane, charming, bewildered as to why we might think that he was involved in anything untoward. You know the type. As soon as his solicitor arrived he shut up shop and, as I say, one phone call later..."

"And you let it drop?"

"Bloody right I did. This place is like snakes and ladders, Detective Sergeants spend all their time climbing their way up the ladders and, oddly enough, are loath to find themselves sitting on a snake sliding back down to the starting point."

"Nevertheless, if there are corrupt practices..."

"I am not saying that there are or there aren't. All I am saying is that I am not in a good position to find out."

"Do you remember anything about the case?"

"I remember that it involved Polish Zlotys and I remember that some large investment fund was involved but apart from that..."

"You don't remember the name of the fund?"

"I knew you were going to ask me that" Davies scratched his head "It was a German-sounding name. That was the reason it was dropped. If this fund was involved it had to be legit because of their governance standards whatever that means"

"Reichenbach?" Davis had seen the name on Craddock's file.

"That's the one. Reichenbach."

England for the English

As Sharon rounded the corner, her phone rang. The dashboard display showed her - it was Jana. Her heart sank. "Hello Jana. What's up?"

"Sorry Sharon. It has happened again. She won't let me in"

"Can't you use the key box?"

"No. She has put on the lock. She is standing by the window calling me names."

"I am on my way, Jana. I will be with you in about ten minutes"

"Good. She says she has called the police."

Minutes later Sharon pulled up in front of the patrol car outside her mother's house.

A young police constable was trying to conduct a conversation with her mother through the lounge window. Jana was standing by the police car while another officer spoke on the radio. Jana was distressed.

"Good. You are here. I am called a foreign whore. I am arrested."

Sharon introduced herself to the policewoman and explained the situation. "This is my mother's carer. She comes every day for an hour to look after her."

"Shit," said the policewoman pithily "So she wasn't trying to break in."

"No," said Jana "Like I said. I have a key but the old woman has put the lock on and calls me names."

The other policeman came over warily. "I can't make her see sense. I need to check if there are any other intruders."

"She is a carer Brian, not an intruder. She has come to look after the old girl."

"Oh bollocks. You mean she is a nutter?"

Sharon bridled. "No. She is my mother and she is just a bit confused."

Brian did not look amused. "False alarm then"

Sharon nodded.

"Best be on our way"

* * *

The hotel lounge was cool after the sun outside. Jasmine was sitting at the table using her phone when Mickey arrived. She motioned for him to wait while she finished her call, then rose gracefully and kissed him on the lips, taking him by surprise.

"Who was that on the phone?" he asked suspiciously

"I was talking to Derek. He sends his regards by the way."

Mickey took a step back "He knows about this?"

"Of course. Why so frightened?" she said "I do what I like. Derek doesn't own me. Anyway, you came. You can't be that scared of him."

"I'm not." Mickey was affronted. He guessed that she was testing him. "I don't know what the food is like here," he said, changing the subject.

She looked at him coolly "I didn't come here to eat."

His mouth felt suddenly dry "What would you like to drink then?" he croaked.

She held his gaze just long enough to make her point. "They do a decent Chablis here but get the whole bottle. I don't want to drink from one that was opened yesterday evening."

She sat back at the table and picked up her phone while Mickey strode off to the bar.

* * *

Sharon and Jana watched as the police got into the patrol car and drove off unnecessarily fast as if making the point that they had been interrupted in their busy schedule. Sharon walked slowly up the steps. "Mum. It's Sharon. Can you open the door please?"

The deadbolt slid back with an audible click, By the time she had unlocked the latch her mother was sitting in the lounge watching the television. It was amazing how quickly she could move when she wanted to thought Sharon. She knew that it would be useless picking her up on her behaviour but she was angry and embarrassed.

"What was that all about?" Her mother was showing an intense interest in a rerun of the Antiques Roadtrip. Sharon seized the remote control and turned it off.

"I said what was all that about? Jana has come to help you and she says you were calling her names."

"She is a liar," Sharon's mother said defiantly "Like all of them"

"Them? Who are them? I want you to apologise to Jana."

"Never," she said, turning her face away.

Jana shrugged. "It was not the first time. I will go and make tea."

As soon as Jana was out of earshot Sharon turned on her mother.

"I am disgusted with you. All she is trying to do is help you out and you behave like a complete moron."

"She shouldn't be here. None of them should. Messing up the NHS. England for the English."

"That rather proves my point, doesn't it? Do you know where Jana comes from?"

"She is a foreigner. Brexit means Brexit"

"She comes from Coventry. Her father was a Polish airman that came here to help fight in the war. Her mother is Welsh. She is as English as you or I."

"Messing up our NHS," said the old woman truculently. "Brexit means Brexit."

"So you said. You also called her a whore. Why was that?"

"She kissed him - the black one."

"That will be her husband. Any idea where he comes from?"

"The EU" the old woman hissed. "They should all go back to where they came from."

"In his case that would be Croydon, I believe." Sharon's anger was building. "Far from messing it up, Jana and her husband are supporting the NHS by looking after old crones like you."

Sharon could see the tears beginning to well up in her mother's eyes. "You are cruel to me. You wish I wasn't here."

"you should be careful what you wish for. If everyone went back to where they came from there wouldn't be anyone left to wipe your backside. I don't wish you weren't here. I just wish you were a normal rational human being."

Her mother was crying soundlessly as Jana brought in the tray of tea.

"Would you like a biscuit? These are Rogaliki. My aunt brought them from Krakow." As if by magic the tears disappeared. "You liked them before" The old woman beamed.

"Thank you, dear. This is my daughter - Megan"

Sharon shut her eyes. "It is Sharon mum. Megan is in Australia."

"Megan always looks after me."

Jana motioned with her head "Cigarette time?"

* * *

Mickey put the wine bucket down on the table and poured two glasses of Chablis. Jasmine, smiling, sipped it. "Sit down next to me," she said patting the space beside her. "Closer"

"You seem to know your way around this place," he said conversationally.

"Let's begin again," she said, "We seem to have got off on the wrong foot". He started as her hand caressed his thigh. "Still so nervous"

"I just wasn't expecting things to move so fast"

"When I see something I want, I have to have it" she leaned over so her lips were almost touching his cheek. "I booked a room when I arrived"

Mickey looked around the lounge expecting to see a sound crew or, worse, some of Derek Sanderson's friends waiting for him to make a false move but there was nobody there. He took a deep breath.

"Shall I bring the wine?" He had meant it to sound masculine and nonchalant, instead, it sounded like a plea.

"Of course," she said and led him out of the lounge.

* * *

They stood on the terrace looking at the rundown back garden. "Thank you for defending me," said Jana "but it is useless. She has forgotten already."

"This garden used to be immaculate when Dad was alive." Sharon could see him kneeling on the lawn planting begonias in the bed that ran down the side of the garden. "He would come home from work and be straight out into the garden. There would always be something to do. A bit of planting. A bit of deadheading. She would be in the kitchen making tea. Bread and Jam. We would all sit down together to eat Megan, me, mum and dad."

"Happy times. I had the same. Fish and chips on a Saturday evening for tea. Papa said one of the best things about England was the fish and chips. My mother died a few years ago and he couldn't cope on his own. I had to put him in a home. You should think of this."

The idea filled Sharon with horror. "Surely she is not that bad is she?"

"It's better for her. People to look after her all the time. She is starting to need this. At the moment she can dress and feed herself but her short-term memory is gone. Did you get the results of the scan?"

"Not yet. It was only three working days ago. They say up to ten."

"Ten days could make all the difference if there is a problem."

"Irrespective, she wants to stay in her own home"

"So did papa - but it is unrealistic when you need so much help"

"I could do more for her. I could come round more often."

"but it is not enough. It will never be enough. Already she makes you angry when she is a silly old woman. If you are here more you are angry more often. It doesn't help her – or you."

Sharon shrugged. "I will think about it. How is your father getting on?"

"He died a couple of months ago. He was in a home for two years. It's about average."

Sharon was filled with a sudden feeling of doom. She couldn't envisage her mother not being around, however infuriating she was. "Only two years. I didn't know."

"You should think about it. Let me know. I can recommend some nice homes."

* * *

Mickey was dazed by the violence of Jasmine's lovemaking. He watched as she dressed her lithe body quickly. "Do you have to go? I thought we could.." his voice tailed off.

"I have to run an errand for Derek." Jasmine was adjusting her makeup.

97

"But..." he began weakly

"Mickey this was always going to be just a quick shag. Considering that you thought we were just going to have a drink, you must be pleased with the outcome."

"I thought we could get to know each other a bit better."

"Yes, and I could come and meet your mum and everything would be sweetness and small fluffy kittens. Sorry, Mickey, I am not that sort of girl."

"I can see that"

"Next time perhaps we will have more time to explore each other but now I have to go. The room is booked for the night if you want to stay."

"Next time?" he asked almost plaintively

"I will ring you," she said as she walked out of the door.

As he lay there his mind wandered onto what exploring more of Jasmine might mean.

Gatwick

Davies had always hated airports. Flying didn't bother him particularly - just hanging around in airports. The channel tunnel had been a godsend as far as holidays were concerned. Put the car on a train and then drive off again at the other end.

When Butler broke the news that they were meeting this Spanish investigator at Gatwick his heart sank and, true to form, here he was - hanging around in an airport lounge.

The arrivals board flickered into life. Flight AZ7641 from Malaga was on the ground - at last.

"Now all we have to do is wait for the border guards to get their thumbs out of their arses and process the passengers" he grumbled.

Butler looked up briefly from the file he was studying and smiled. "Another hour then." Davies groaned. "Speaking of the border force, did you ever get any info from them about Sanderson? It would be nice to know if his little stay in Spain was just a one-off or a regular jaunt."

Davies laughed. "No. Apparently, it is a real pain for them to pull off specific information so all requests have to go through at the very top before they will consider it.

The Spanish on the other hand are right on the ball. Their records show him travelling in and out of Malaga on four separate occasions in the last year."

"So he has been a busy boy." Butler made a note on the file. "or he plays a lot of golf in the sun. Did you find us a room for this meeting or are we slumming it in the lounge?"

"I will go and talk to my contact. He promised to find us something" Davies stalked off.

Passengers began to emerge through the automatic doors. The first flush of businessmen in a hurry were gathered in by placard-wielding drivers standing behind the rope barrier.

Couples clasping plastic bags full of cheap booze and cigarettes. Small, sleepy children being shepherded by bickering parents. Finally a looming shape that he recognised escorting a dapper, youthful man with black hair who stood apart from the rest of the crowd. Butler recognised something about him instantly - he exuded authority.

Toro bounded across the concourse. "Mr Butler. Great to see you again." He seized Butler's hand and shook it vigorously. "This is the chief – Judge Rojo – Detective Butler."

Rojo nodded and shook Butler's hand just warmly enough "A pleasure to meet you." Butler heard hardly a trace of an accent. "We are looking forward to working with you on this little project."

"Happy to be of some assistance" Butler felt irrationally flustered by Rojo's slickness and easy manner. "I am sure criminality knows no boundaries"

Rojo smiled winningly "and criminals certainly don't. We have had our fair share of your villains over the years. Toro was telling me how you met."

It was Butler's turn to smile. "It was a big bust that one."

"Our loss was Northern Cyprus' gain"

* * *

The meeting room was small and airless. Rojo was in full flow. "The remit of my team is to investigate institutional corruption which, I am sad to say, is a growth stock. Because it tends to be political, we work apart from other investigators and only involve them where we need extra pairs of hands for example.

The reason I am telling you this is because if you decide to help us you will find that we are not lovers of what you might call normal channels. Everything about this is a state secret in Spain and I need to know that you will keep any information that we share confidential in that context. "

Butler nodded "We understand the need for secrecy"

Davies looked puzzled "So if this is all being done on the sly how does it ever make it to court? Rules of evidence and so on..."

Rojo smiled again " A very valid point. Although I am a judge I only have a limited ability to vary such rules so we have to make sure that we have concrete evidence against these people."

"Don't you have people you report to?"

"In theory, at least the only person who can remove me from my post is his Royal Majesty the king. So I guess I report to him."

Davies raised an eyebrow.

"Let me introduce you to our main suspect" Rojo continued, flashing up a picture on his laptop "Juan Mijas. He is a prominent local politician and businessman in Andalusia and has a lot of political influence regionally.

We have substantial evidence that Senor Mijas is abusing his position as Mayor to grant building permits to developers in

101

return for money. He doesn't act alone in this. We believe that his head of what you would call planning is complicit and, much as it pains me to say so, he also has a judge on his payroll."

Photographs of the meeting at the restaurant flashed up as Rojo was speaking.

"They don't appear to have been keeping their relationship a secret."

Rojo smiled "Indeed no. The arrogance of power I think."

"They think they are untouchable"

"They may think so, but Inspector Toro's team is working to uncover a paper trail linking each of them with payments. Once we have done that we can investigate the legality of each transfer."

"Are you able to identify the origin of these payments?"

"Certainly. There are many of them over the last few years but the most recent was from an account in Gibraltar. Relations with Gibraltar being a little strained, we have been unable to verify the account holder formally.

Informally it belongs to a company - Trizer 77 limited. Incorporated in the Cayman Islands and, apparently, still live."

Butler looked at Davies quizzically. What had all been a Spanish problem alone had suddenly veered in his direction. "Does that ring any bells?"

After his many years of service Davies had a well-developed avoidance reflex. "Not immediately. I will ask around."

Rojo smiled again. "As you will know, the Cayman islands is particularly difficult to penetrate in terms of information.

Fortunately, we have some contacts there and we have identified a link between Trizer 77 and a company called Reichenbach, who, we are led to believe, is the sole owner."

Davies was a terrible card player. Despite many years trying to hide his tells, his face showed surprise and then interest.

"You are familiar with the name?"

It was Butler's turn to be defensive. Thus far they had uncovered no evidence linking Sanderson or his company with any criminality. He had no record, paid his taxes on time and had a long track record of successful development around the world.

"Reichenbach may relate to a person of interest to us in a number of investigations going back several years."

"I would be interested to hear about this person of interest." Rojo sat back expectantly.

"It is a bit early in our investigation to name names"

"Perhaps we can be of assistance. Inspector Toro obtained a passenger list for all the Malaga flights around the meeting time. Amongst the travellers was a Mr Derek Sanderson.

Is he not the Managing Director of the Reichenbach asset management company?"

Davies was mildly furious. "That was a lucky break." Unlike his face, his voice portrayed no emotion at all.

Butler cut across him "Inspector Toro and I have discussed Derek Sanderson. Although we have suspicions about criminal activity on his behalf we have no firm evidence.

How strong is the link between Reichenbach and Trizer 77?"

Rojo pursed his lips. "It is in the public domain – or what passes for it in the Caymans. Our contact is usually reliable. All he did was give us the name and I am relying upon his expertise.

Am I sure there is a link? If he says so, of course.

Can I prove it? No. Am I likely to be able to get formal evidence of a link? I doubt it."

Toro watched the proceedings with interest. His English was not honed enough to pick up all the nuances of the conversation but he could see from the expressions of the two Englishmen that they had been unsettled by the information.

The Sergeant looked as though he would cheerfully throttle Rojo given the chance. He could hold back no more.

"We are on the same side in this." All three men looked at him with surprise. "If this Sanderson comes again to Spain I will arrest him myself."

Butler smiled "That is nice to know but we need to make sure that when you do that he cannot wriggle off your hook.

Since you have been so open with us may I share what we know?"

Rojo nodded "Please"

"We at the National Crime Agency have been following a particular money laundering operation for some time. As part of that investigation, we identified a company that might be involved – Estados Developments.

When this same company opened a shop in Brighton, we became more interested.

As I am sure you know, the real estate sector is prone to having lots of cash sloshing around - in the form of deposits taken on developments, for example. We suspect that these deposits are unlikely to be used for their original purpose.

We have noticed the involvement of one Michael Fisher who is known to us as a low-level fraudster. Intelligence, but crucially no evidence, points to the involvement of Derek Sanderson, an altogether bigger fish, with links to our original investigation.

His company, Reichenbach, appear to be the owners of Estados Developments. At this point, it is worth saying that, so far, we have little evidence of wrongdoing."

Rojo broke his silence "Do you have enough evidence to intervene? Interrogate perhaps?"

"Not yet, but we will have. Thus far we have been letting Fisher carry on in the expectation that he will incriminate himself. When we arrest him, we will use that criminality as leverage to uncover the link to Reichenbach and Derek Sanderson.

Given that Sanderson features in a much bigger operation I am reluctant to make him aware of our interest just yet but your input has been most helpful."

Rojo nodded. "Equally I don't want to prejudice your investigation by acting precipitately to make arrests at our end.

We need to keep in close touch and, with luck, we can net the whole shoal rather than a few small fish."

* * *

They watched as the two men strolled off to catch their return flight. "I reckon," said Davies "That if we play our cards right, our next meeting should be over there not over here"

Butler smiled. "I have to brave the shark-infested waters of Smallbone's office to arrange that"

"What was all that bollocks about the National Crime Agency? I thought you were just replacing Buckland"

"Sorry" Butler grimaced "Sometimes these things have to be on a need to know basis"

"and I didn't need to know. Nice"

Lunch

Liszt was playing softly in the background as Toro entered the restaurant. He worked the room expertly with his eyes, searching out any nooks and crannies where danger might lurk.

The restaurant was reasonably busy with businessmen no doubt discussing the state of the market before slipping off for a siesta. Hector Diamante was already seated in a booth away from the window as requested. Toro noted his presence but he gave no sign that he had seen him.

The head waiter intercepted him. "The microphone is live. The kitchen is clear and secure as are the lavatories. Do you want to check?"

Being a few metres from the Supreme Court, the Fernando was well used to the security needs of important people. Toro put his head around the kitchen door. The frenetic activity should indicate that the threats were limited from that quarter. He opened the lavatory door and quickly checked the empty stalls much to the discomfort of a middle-aged gentleman emptying his bladder at the urinal. He raised his radio. "OK Judge," He said quietly.

Rojo entered the restaurant soundlessly and made his way to the booth. Toro positioned himself at the table reserved for him with a commanding view of the entrances, adjusted his earpiece and checked the recorder.

Diamante rose to his feet. "Jesus" he smiled "It has been a long time. When did I last see you?".

Rojo shook his hand. "It must have been five years ago at that conference in Paris."

"As long ago as that? Sit, please. I am surprised that our paths don't cross more often."

"Not so surprising. After all, I have little to do with civil matters."

Diamante feigned surprise. "Of course. You concentrate entirely on criminal cases."

"Indeed, but I wondered if I might pick your brains on a civil matter?"

Rojo knew Hector Diamante from his days at law school. Their time there didn't overlap but Diamante had lectured there regularly as a respected alumnus. He remembered a good speaker, rich with anecdotes but tempered with a vanity and a preference for the sound of his voice over others.

"Shall we order first? Then I will do what I can to help."

Toro studied Diamante intently. If he had any suspicions he was hiding them well. To anyone looking in it was as if two old friends were having a convivial lunch together. He directed the waiter, joking with him about his knowledge of the wine list, the quality of seafood so far from the ocean and the tenderness of the pork loin. The waiter smiled and demurred in pursuit of a decent tip. Rojo watched and waited for the bluster to pass.

"What do you think of a Basque fish stew as a main course. I don't get to Barcelona enough but when I do..."

"Delicious" Rojo nodded.

"and a bottle of Rioja Blanco – the 2015 vintage."

As he left the waiter caught Toro's eye. "What an arsehole" he murmured. It was Toro's turn to smile. Once the starters had been delivered he stopped at the table.

"What can I get you?"

"Just a selection of tapas and a glass of water please, no gas"

The waiter made a note. "Enough gas for the whole restaurant over there"

Rojo waited for Diamante to take a mouthful of his clams. "The matter on which I need your advice is one of civil planning, which, I believe is one of your specialities?"

Diamante nodded, unable to speak with his mouth full.

"It seems like local officials may have been taking inducements to grant building permits in a national park."

Diamante swallowed quickly "Really? Surely bribing an official is a criminal matter."

"Indeed, as is accepting a bribe in public office but I just wanted to get the planning law straight in my mind before I move on to the next stage."

Diamante pushed his starter to one side half-eaten. "This is a complex area" he began, spreading out his hands. Rojo could see himself back in law school listening intently at the master class.

"At the top level, the Constitution says that the public authorities will watch over the rational utilization of natural resources and this forms the legislative basis for setting conditions on the activities of individuals and the approach to enforcement. The authority, in this case, lies with the regional administration although the ministry can become involved in more difficult cases or where the crime takes place in more than one region."

Diamante was in full flow. Toro was mesmerized by his extravagant hand gestures and the way he emphasized different points. He had been well trained to spot bluffers and chancers in the course of interrogation and, even from across the restaurant, he could smell the bullshit.

"However much the authorities might seek to encourage the taking of preventive action, there are criminal as well as civil remedies. As you will know the penal code was modified to include environmental crime and the worst cases can result in imprisonment."

"So, if I may take stock" Rojo was tiring of the lecture. "Clearly, the officials taking the bribes are committing an offence. The developers offering the bribes are committing an offence and then compounding that by committing a civil and criminal environmental crime by actually building in a protected area. It is also clear that anyone acting with knowledge of those crimes is also committing an offence of conspiracy at least."

Diamante nodded sagely. "It sounds as though there could be a long charge sheet in this case. Can you tell me any more about it?"

"I would rather tighten up the evidence before I go public. I can tell you that it relates to the Andalusia region but you understand it is quite sensitive, particularly as the corruption seems to extend quite a long way up the tree."

"So why are Seville not dealing with this?" The hands moved out palm upwards questioningly "Surely the whole idea of regional courts is to cover off things in their jurisdiction?"

Rojo took a mouthful of *croqueta* before answering. "You see, Judge, our investigations have uncovered a conspiracy that cuts across regional and indeed national boundaries. We have evidence of links to the judiciary and to the UK which, we believe, is the source of funds for the enterprise. I returned from London yesterday after some interesting discussions with Inspector Butler of their National Crime Agency."

Diamante shook his head slowly "Be careful who you pick as enemies Jesus Rojo. You are getting something of a reputation for tilting at windmills."

Rojo cocked his head quizzically. "If the windmills are corrupt then they need to be demolished and rebuilt"

"Just make sure that they don't fall on you in the process. Powerful people have powerful friends who are fond of direct action." Toro eased the strap of his holster open, making the weapon visible at his hip. For a man like Diamante that was as close as it got to a direct threat.

Rojo smiled. "Generally, I am well protected. Even at lunch"

The amiable Diamante disappeared as quickly as it had been assumed. Stony-faced he scanned the restaurant. Toro met his gaze and saw the fire burning within. He adjusted his earpiece ostentatiously.

"You are recording this?" Any hint of jollity in his eyes had been replaced by pure venom but, for the moment, the politesse remained. "You know that nothing you have recorded can be used against me. "

Rojo raised his eyebrows "and what have you said Judge that you want to unsay?"

Finally the anger moved the polite façade aside. "This is deliberate entrapment Rojo." He shouted. "You know the supreme court rules on illicit recording. Your masters won't be able to save you from censure this time." He rose to his feet grandly - the serviette still tucked into his shirt ruining the dramatic effect.

Rojo leaned back in his chair "Before you go, Judge, know this. My officers are very thorough. We have photographic evidence of all the key players in this crime and we will be interviewing shortly. Our next discussion may well be under caution."

Diamante snorted and stormed away from the table. Toro stood up as Diamante approached his table his bulk looming over the enraged judge who stood inches from him glowering. "You... You are an accomplice to this" He hissed and marched out of the restaurant.

Toro shrugged his shoulders and eased his gun back into its holster. "I have been called worse"

"Thank you Toro" Rojo was satisfied.

"That is a wrap. You had better join me. We have some *marmitako* arriving soon and it would be a shame to waste it."

* * *

112

Rio was pleased. Finding Scott MacDonald's details had not been as difficult as she had feared. A local newsagent identified him immediately as the famous footballer to whom he delivered English newspapers every day and had even provided him with a signed picture of him wearing his football kit.

She found herself a spot sitting outside a café opposite an upmarket block of flats just away from the city centre. She watched as people went into and came out of the building. The MacDonald apartment was on the top floor but of the man himself, there was no sign.

She finished her sandwich, drained her espresso and walked over to the entrance. A woman pulling a small suitcase on wheels waved her access card and the door clicked open. Rio held it open while she struggled in with the suitcase and they both walked to the lift.

"I am looking for the apartment of Scott MacDonald," Rio said speculatively as she pressed the button for the top floor and the lift began to rise "I don't suppose you could direct me."

The woman looked at her suspiciously. "He is my boyfriend. What do you want to see him about?"

The lift doors opened and Rio stood back to let her pass. "A lost access card," she said. The woman's expression changed as she looked towards the apartment and she stifled a cry.

Rio stepped swiftly out of the lift. The door was hanging off at a drunken angle. "Police," she said, "Stay here" and, gun drawn, she approached the flat.

It didn't take long to check that everywhere was clear. It had been turned over professionally and messily – papers were strewn everywhere including, Rio noticed, a passport. He could hear crying from the hallway as the woman surveyed the scene.

"Who would do this?" she asked before staggering and collapsing. Rio caught her before she fell and sat her down on a sofa that had remained upright.

Rio retrieved an intact mug from the wreckage of the kitchen and gave her some water to sip. "I am sorry," she said "It was such a shock. Scottie will be horrified. You said you were the police?"

"Yes," said Rio "but I am from the CNP, not the local force. When did you last speak to Scottie? Sorry, I didn't catch your name."

"It is Inez. I last spoke to him a week ago. I have been in Barcelona visiting my family. I thought he must be at home. I rang his work to tell him I was back and they said that they haven't seen him for days."

"Where does he work?"

"At the municipal centre."

She began to cry soundlessly and clung to Rio for comfort. "Something has happened to him. I am sure of it."

"Don't worry. People drop off the radar for a while all the time. A few drinks turn into a few more..... He will probably walk through the door any minute."

"He doesn't drink" Inez sobbed "He doesn't even take aspirin if he can avoid it."

After a while, the sobbing ceased and she blew her nose noisily. "We have only been together for just over a year," she said wiping her eyes, "I told him to be careful but he was so pig-headed. They did this."

"Who did this?"

"Mayor Mijas and his criminals."

Rio looked at her earnestly "Can I ask you some questions now or would you prefer to come to the police station later and make a statement?"

"No. Not the police station. They will find out."

"So tell me why Mayor Mijas would burgle your apartment."

Inez took a sip from the mug of water "Scottie works for Mayor Mijas and has done ever since the football. He was a good player. He played for Glasgow I think and when Mijas took over the club he bought him as a star. 'Big Mac' they called him but he got injured and couldn't play again so Mijas gave him a job in his office."

"So why search his flat?" Rio was mystified. She half-remembered the story of the star footballer from the newspapers.

"Scottie was a clever man. He had studied computers while he was playing football and he didn't like what he found when he was working for the Mayor. So he began to make copies of files. He was going to go to the papers. They must have found out."

"Do you know what he found?"

"No, but it was something to do with illegal payments."

Rio could see why the flat had been thoroughly searched "Did he keep copies of the files here?"

"They were on his computer – but they have taken it"

Rio cursed inwardly.

"There is something else. Before I left for Barcelona, Scottie gave me this memory stick." She began to cry again. "He said if anything happens I should give it to Greg Matthews."

"You would do better to let me have it," said Rio, putting it in her pocket "Mister Matthews is in hospital at the moment. He also got too close to Mayor Mijas." She was starting to get a bad feeling. "So, your boyfriend didn't drink, didn't take drugs?" Inez shook her head. "Does he have any places he could hide?"

"I can't think of anywhere. Our best friends are Greg and Mary Matthews. We go out with them sometimes. He has no relatives in Spain and hasn't kept in touch with the football team."

"Does he have any means of getting about? A car perhaps?"

"Yes. The car park is in the basement. Bay 27"

"I will check if the car is still there. Are you OK to stay here?"

She shook her head again. "I will show you the way."

A red Fiat was sitting untouched in Bay 27.

"I will get a forensic team to give it the once over to see if we can find out where he has gone."

"Perhaps he has taken my car." She indicated the vacant space in the next bay. "Why would he do that?"

"OK," said Rio "I need to put out a call. What is the colour, make and registration number?"

"It is a white Mazda MX5 - I don't remember the registration."

Naughty boys

The view from the terrace was spectacular. On the bank opposite, the City of London spread outwards and upwards. The menacing bulk of HMS Belfast stood as if guarding the ebb and flow of money in and around the institutions headquartered there. Butler stood waiting as the heavily built detective paced back and forth listening on his phone. Eventually, he hung up and walked over.

"You were right to be suspicious. Reichenbach own lots of real estate and we have been watching them for a couple of years. The outfit is run by Sanderson who we suspect of all kinds of bad things. My governor is not keen for you to go anywhere near him unless you have evidence of significant money laundering activity. Even then he wants a commitment that you will hand over that evidence to us in fraud and back off. Do you have any evidence?"

Butler laughed "Would I be here if I had?"

"What do you think he is up to?"

"We have a grubby little deposit-taking scam operating on our patch. On the face of it, they sell the lifestyle, show them plans for a development then skedaddle when they have their hands on a healthy deposit. So far so small beer. A couple of things make this different. Firstly, the development company seems legit with the backing of Reichenbach; secondly, our friend Sanderson was spotted by our Spanish chums in conversation with their main suspects in a corruption investigation."

"Corruption covers a multitude of sins. What has he been doing?"

"We are not sure but the guy that the Spanish are investigating may be selling planning permissions."

"For developments like the one your targets are selling. He really is a naughty boy, isn't he. Nevertheless, be very careful if you go near him. We don't want to pinch him for stealing sweets when he is lifting the whole shop."

"Understood. It seems odd that he keeps appearing on the radar. The NCA know about him. You at fraud have a file on him. I am sure the spooks will have a file on him yet he is still at it and nobody seems to be able to stop him."

"My response to that would be – yet. He will make a mistake one of these days and then we will have him. There is something else you should be aware of. What level of security clearance do you have?"

Butler was surprised by the question "SC. I was vetted three months ago for a project with GCHQ"

"Good. I am amongst friends. What brought Reichenbach to our attention initially was a laundering project in Jamaica a couple of years ago. I won't bore you with all the details, you can look them up when you get back to the ranch, but whatever the file says it was a lot worse, involved Government ministers and the key suspects all ended up very dead along with two of our officers. As soon as we got close we found we had specials all over us like a rash looking for terrorist connections. So, when I say be careful, I mean it. Sanderson is very smooth and clubbable but there are other things in play. Reichenbach is ruthless and very, very nasty when things don't go their way."

"Do you have anything on their Cayman Islands connection?"

"Other than that they are registered there not really. It is very common for these big funds with global interests to register in a tax haven. Not only does it save them a fortune in tax but it shields them from scrutiny.

"How does it work?"

"Typically, a local lawyer acts as their agent, setting up companies, filing returns and so on. There is no need for them ever to set foot in the place."

"And we have no leverage with these lawyers at all?"

"None. Like every other police force, we have contacts in the Caymans. Like every other police force, our enquiries go nowhere. Funny that."

* * *

Mickey parked the Jag in the public car park across the way and walked down to the lockup. The door seemed secure, no one had been trying to get in. He had already checked the CCTV on-line but he believed that you could never be too careful – this was his biggest secret. Not even Sharon had an inkling of its existence.

Inside, it was comfortable enough. Years ago he had insulated and draught-proofed the garage and installed a bed. There was no shower but the municipal swimming baths were only five minutes away.

He moved the filing cabinet and opened the safe set in the floor. He didn't need the money or the passports yet – but he always checked that they were there. This was his escape route. If everything went pear-shaped he would grab the contents and disappear.

He wondered about where he would go. Where would Jasmine go? He fancied hiding in plain sight but it would have to be somewhere with better weather than Brighton.

* * *

Sanderson watched as they assembled, analysts, investors and journalists each clutching their glass of champagne. Most investment lunches saw cheap fizz being handed out but not at Reichenbach. This was a 2009 Le Brun that he had chosen himself. It amused him that the ripe apple flavours would, of course, be wasted on most of the audience – but they would love being spoilt. The fund had a reputation for being the best and it was that part of the brand that he was keen to polish. The better people think you are - the better you become, he reasoned.

They looked, he thought, pathetically grateful for the crumbs being offered. Yet, being in the investment business, they should know that everything has, at some stage, to be paid for. Their fine wine served in crystal flutes was coming off the returns that they were so eager to see maintained as were the concoctions of the celebrity chef hired for the occasion.

He hadn't given much thought to his presentation. He had agreed to talk about risk – a subject that governed almost all his daily life. In truth it was his addiction and, like all addictions, it was proving increasingly difficult to control. Criminality was just another set of risks that he factored into any decision, not that he would be talking about that.

The dependence on risk ran through him like a seam. From games of chicken on the railway when he was a boy, racing motorbikes in his teens through to high returning investments now. They all made his pulse race.

Risk was a subject with which most of his audience should be achingly familiar as its impact on their profitability, and therefore bonuses, was huge. Sadly though, they didn't understand it at all. Risk had a taste and a smell all of its own. Their view of risk was heavily influenced by consensus. If any particular type of asset was agreed to be safe – then safe it became and dissenting voices were overwhelmed by the ensuing silence. He could feel risk in his fingertips and price it accordingly.

"The slides are all ready to go. Do you need anything else?" Jasmine waited expectantly. He smiled. He liked Jasmine. He would almost go as far as trusting her but she was her own woman and however much she might tolerate him and his addictions, she would always be looking out for herself. Ivana hated her, of that he was certain, feeling that her place in his bed was being usurped. This was not without some truth – they had sex regularly – but he realised early on that Jasmine used sex as a means to an end.

"How did it go with Fisher?" he asked quietly

"Everything under control" she smiled "He is shit scared of you. He couldn't get his head around the fact that you knew I was meeting him. He took a bit of warming up but I left him wanting more."

He smiled. "Keep him on the leash. He may yet prove useful."

"Looks like we have a full house – all waiting to hear from their guru."

"I was thinking that I might tell them that we are going to sell all our equities and invest the money in gun-running to the Middle East. Do you think they would applaud?"

"They wouldn't like the short term dip in returns – but long-term...." She smiled

"Let's do this," he said and, with Jasmine at his side, moved through the double doors into the auditorium.

* * *

"Do you have anything on Sanderson personally?"

"I haven't had the pleasure but they say he is driven and hates losing at anything. His file is pretty thick. I'll make sure you get a copy so you can pick through looking for weaknesses just like we have been doing for the past two years."

Butler was determined not to be brushed off "Where did he go to school? Which university? First girlfriend or boyfriend?"

The detective held up his hands "OK. OK. Every so often the posh public schools allow a few plebs in to be buggered by the prefects. Our Derek came from a council estate in West London and managed to get one of those scholarships to Eton.

Star pupil. Did well in his exams. Went on to Oxford where he studied medieval history believe it or not. He was a bit of a risk junkie at Uni - broke his leg badly hang-gliding while he was there but still got a first.

His first job was at a big management consultancy where he became a star all over again. Joined Reichenbach ten years ago when they were an also-ran in the fund world. Within five years he was CEO and they had become top dollar. The bloke is well connected. There was a do at his place in the country that we were watching. He had MPs, dignitaries, celebs even your new boss Proudfoot all eating his food and drinking his wine."

"Proudfoot?"

"Yes. Sensitive area. To cover our backs with the anti-corruption stasi we did some digging. He and Sanderson are best buddies on the golf course which asks some questions about his position."

"Indeed it does. I'll file that one for future reference"

"Very wise. It is always nice to have one up the barrel for a rainy day. I don't think I have left anything out."

Butler smiled "First girlfriend?"

"Oh yeah. Married young to a university friend whose name I can't remember. Divorced five or six years ago and married Ivana, an absolute corker by the way, who comes from Russia. Not Russia, Kyiv. Two daughters."

"Very impressive. Kyiv is in Ukraine by the way"

"Oh and he is shagging his secretary, Jasmine something. Who is another stunner by the way. I wonder how he gets away with it. I mean he's no fucking oil painting is he."

"Money," said Butler "and power. They win every time"

* * *

Mickey was preoccupied. While he had been setting it up, the project was exciting and he had spent every waking hour planning, organizing and executing. Now it was happening he was bored. He wasn't cut out for a managerial role – he was more of a man of action.

From his office, he could see Sharon talking on the phone. She was a good-looker and he loved the way that her blond hair fell over the side of her face as she chatted away. She was working hard but he knew she was struggling with her mother. She was taking the next day off to look at care homes and had wanted him to go with her. He had invented a meeting to get out of it.

She reached over to pick up something from the printer and he could see her breasts straining against her blouse. She still had a hell of a body but... The buts became ever louder the more he thought of Jasmine. She too had a hell of a body, more androgynous but also more flexible and she knew how to use it.

The problem was what to do about Sharon. It seemed like they had been together forever and he was bored with that too. He wasn't brave enough to just dump her, especially if they were still working together. He had already started to move some of his stuff out of the house to his lockup. If push came to shove he could always kip down there temporarily.

Very shortly he would have to shut down the Brighton operation and Sharon would have to find a new job. That would be the best time for a clean break leaving the field clear for Jasmine.

He hadn't come to any conclusion as to why Jasmine was interested in him when clearly, she had a rich sugar daddy in Sanderson. He wondered if he was being manipulated but couldn't see why and dismissed the idea. He didn't understand why she had told Sanderson that they were meeting.

Perhaps he was one of those old pervs who got off on watching. He wondered if their exploits had been filmed – he didn't want to become an internet porn star although he had nothing to be ashamed of. No. She was probably just bored with the same old missionary position and wanted to branch out. What was it she said – explore each other. He looked forward to that.

Danny La Rue

The smell was hard to categorise. Elements of ammonia combined with furniture polish seemed about right. Overall, it gave the impression of decay. The entrance hall was gloomy despite being lit from above. A large mahogany staircase rose into the bowels of the building. An old man clutching an aluminium walking frame stood to attention by the side of the doorway. "Name?" he barked, causing Sharon to flinch involuntarily. "Business?"

Sharon forced a weak smile.

"Don't mind him," said the nurse. "Are you feeling OK Mr Flanaghan?"

"Flanaghan. Sergeant. 274531"

"Carry on Sergeant. " The nurse turned back to Sharon. "Mr Flanaghan always guards the entrance. It is all he remembers poor love. My name is Linda. I am the manager here at High Trees. You must be Mrs Fellows."

"Sharon. Mrs Fellows is my mother" Sharon was thrown momentarily. She wasn't Mrs anybody.

"A quick Cook's tour of the facilities first?"

Sharon nodded

"Good, then we can go to my office to discuss your mother."

She led Sharon through the double doors into a sitting room where half a dozen old ladies were sitting each clutching a card and a marker pen. A nurse was sitting at a card table by the window.

"Ready Ladies. The next number is fifty-two"

"Danny La Rue" shrieked one of the old ladies.

"We try and have some kind of activity every day. Sometimes it is bingo, sometimes a quiz. Nothing too demanding. Of course, it is voluntary. Nobody has to participate if they don't want to."

"They all seem to be enjoying themselves"

"Most of them don't know what is going on bless them. We run trips out once a week. We have our own minibus."

They climbed the wide staircase and waited outside a fire door while two carers negotiated the access control system. Sharon was reminded of the time she visited one of her friends in Chelmsford prison.

The room was small, but nice enough with a small window overlooking the gardens.

"This is typical of the kind of room your mother would occupy at High Trees"

"Does it have its own toilet and so on?"

"This one doesn't but our top-up rooms come fully en-suite and some have sea views"

"What is a top-up room?" asked Sharon

"It is a room that costs more than the Local Authority are prepared to pay. I mean if your mother is self-funding then it doesn't apply."

"Sorry. I don't understand any of that"

The nurse smiled indulgently "Let's go to my office."

She led the way down a dingy corridor to a small airless room that appeared to be full of paper. Every surface was covered. She moved a pile of box files off a chair and placed them on the floor. "Every customer is different " she continued "...and we pride ourselves at High Trees that we cater for everyone."

Sharon perched on the chair, trying not to read the papers on the desk. On one of them, someone had scrawled "looney" in red marker. "My mother is struggling at home." she began "even though she has carers coming in every day."

"That is a real shame" the nurse clucked sympathetically. "How old is she now?"

"Seventy-eight" Sharon shuddered involuntarily. Her mother had always kept her real age a secret and was known to lead off alarmingly if the truth were revealed.

The nurse noted it down. "is there any diagnosis?"

Sharon was confused "Diagnosis of what?"

The nurse mouthed dementia soundlessly.

"Dementia?"

"We prefer to call it confusion. We feel it is more positive."

"No formal diagnosis. No, but she can get very forgetful."

"So you wouldn't say she needs nursing care."

"No. Not really"

"No physical disability? She can bear her weight? walk? Feed herself and so on?"

"Yes, she can do all that." It occurred to Sharon that if she could do all those things, why wouldn't she? and why was Sharon here discussing her mother as though she were a second-hand car.

"These are all standard questions I am afraid. I know they sound a bit bureaucratic but we just have to go through the list once then we can concentrate on your mother as a person."

Sharon considered the interaction her mother had had with anyone unfortunate enough to cross her path over the last decade. She was just an average racist, xenophobic Daily Mail reader really, prone to leading off about matters that she felt qualified to give her opinion.

"She has become more withdrawn recently," said Sharon diplomatically.

"No sign of cognitive impairment? She can handle money?"

Sharon nodded. "She won't spend any money."

"That is pretty common with someone of her age. On the subject of money, does she have savings of over £23,500?"

"No. She has a little in the Post Office but nothing like that. She spends all her pension on living."

"Does she own her own property?"

"No," said Sharon. They had transferred it to Sharon and her sister several years ago before their father died.

"Has she ever owned a property?"

"No. She always rented" Sharon lied. She had heard stories about how they would go after the house if it were available.

Linda read the last page of the form "So none of that applies" she said to herself. "Good. It looks like your mother will need local authority funding. That is not something I can arrange for you but I can give you the contacts so that you can arrange it."

Sharon had a feeling of gloom in the pit of her stomach. "What does that entail?" she asked quietly.

Linda moved around the desk and shut the door. "I would be lying if I told you that it was anything other than a pain in the arse," she said. "We just skipped through a list of the main questions that you will be asked, only in much more detail. The Council has no money, nor has the NHS and it is easy to fall down the crack in the middle by giving the wrong answers. The Council will do a financial assessment on your mother and you need to make sure that any money she does have is well hidden. They will want to see everything including bank statements going back three years. If there is evidence that she has disposed of any assets or money they will want to see where it went and when. Of course, I shouldn't be telling you all this."

"Perhaps a care home isn't such a good idea"

"That, of course, is a matter for you and her but remember that nothing changes for the better in this situation. You are reaching the stage where you both will have to resign yourselves to change in the way you live your lives. It is harder for some than for others. Take Mr Flanaghan that you met at the door. He adapted to institutional life very easily but we have others who spend all their time in tears fearing that they have been abandoned by their kids. We are caught in the middle."

Sharon grimaced "I wouldn't want her to think that"

"Of course not, so you need to make sure that she is fully committed to the idea. As far as the Council are concerned you will do yourself no favours by minimising her condition.

You became defensive when I touched on this earlier, it will go better for your mother if you are realistic about her condition, even exaggerating it a little. These people have seen it all before but they have a checklist on which boxes need to be ticked. Unless they are they can do nothing."

* * *

As she sat contemplating High Trees with a large glass of red wine in her hand, it seemed odd that to make sure her mother was cared for she would have to lie about her condition. Her priority now would have to be looking after her.

She looked across at Mickey who was engrossed in the snooker. He had been acting strangely in the last few days. Normally he liked to come home and put his feet up before having a cuddle on the sofa but recently he had been miles away.

She sighed "Mickey. There is something I want to talk about."

He pressed the mute button. "What's this?" he asked

"I am going to pack it in at the shop. Mum is getting worse and I need to look after her"

Mickey raised his eyebrows "OK" he said "I can't pretend it is a surprise. She has been on the slippery slope for some time."

And that was it. No fight. No debate. No attempts to persuade her to change her mind. Something was very wrong.

"By the way," he said "I have to go down to Bristol for a meeting on Thursday. I might have to stay down there."

"Very nice," she said, "a night in a Cotswold hideaway."

"You can come along if you like" Mickey shrugged "but you'll be on your own all day. Will your mum be OK?"

"No. I'll leave it" Sharon backed off. Mickey had played the mother card. Something was seriously wrong.

Press

The bar was loud, too loud, but the beer was cold and it gave Rio the opportunity to marshall her thoughts. Anya was at work which gave her some space to think about what to do about her. Madrid was one option – letting her down gently was the other.

The case had been going in circles before she had uncovered the memory stick which looked like it was the magic key to unlock everything and allow them to get back to Madrid.

She had only glanced over the contents but the files were mostly images of spreadsheets that told the whole story.

There was still the problem of the missing footballer who, no doubt, could provide even more interpretation of the data. She didn't doubt that they would find him, preferably alive. It was very difficult to make yourself completely invisible in a city like Malaga.

"I don't like to see a lady drinking alone" The voice was, she guessed, American. She smiled graciously "Actually, I like drinking alone. That's why I do it."

"Let me buy you a drink. What'll it be?"

He was too drunk to take the hint "Go away" she said nicely.

"Come on. I only want to buy you a drink"

"Go away, please," she said menacingly.

"Just one...." He lost his chain of thought and backed away as Rio drew her service pistol and showed him her badge.

"Go away now" she ordered.

* * *

When Mary was at University, her professor had always tried to put her off a career in proofreading.

"As well as an eye for detail and a shed-load of patience it requires a dark, obsessive personality. Do you have such a personality, Mary? Your behaviour in the college bar suggests to me that you do not!"

As she put the latest edition of the Costa Enquirer to bed, she could hear his words echoing around the empty office. She didn't feel obsessive but she did own up to a stubborn streak that she was relying on to sustain her.

Ever since Greg started to investigate Mayor Mijas, things had been getting worse. It started with people spitting in their direction on the street and muttered insults in the local shops. Then there was the graffiti on Bessie - they awoke one morning to find that someone had scrawled "Go home" in black paint across the windscreen.

Local advertisers had started not returning their calls and withdrawing their copy. Fortunately, the national companies whose wares they promoted were outside the orbit of the Mayor's business acquaintances. Their landlord, who had welcomed them into the redundant office space with open arms, had become much more distant and was talking about repossessing the space for redevelopment.

Since the incident in Malaga when Greg got beaten up there had been a barrage of abuse online including death threats that, frankly, were scaring Mary. Every creak and groan heard in the old building caused her to listen acutely and three times already she had checked that all the doors were locked.

She wished Greg was here, if for no other reason than this was his baby - the culmination of almost two years work. She just hoped that it didn't mean the end of the newspaper. They were running short of resources and the Mayor knew that. There was no doubt that he wouldn't like the headline, the question was what he would do in retaliation.

They had run the lead article past Scottie MacDonald, who was the unnamed source for much of the information, a couple of weeks before. He had seemed jumpy and distant but agreed on the text. She had checked each article and advert for typos. She had checked the layout and to be certain she had checked the advice given to them by Greg's lawyers - the same advice that he had chosen to ignore.

"It just isn't right" he had insisted on his phone from the hospital. "We can't just stand back and watch this happen. It must be stopped."

"What about just giving it to the police? You said that a judge is investigating corruption"

"It all takes too long. Mijas will have retired to Florida by the time they get around to prosecuting him. This will force them to take action."

She clipped the proof for the front page onto the board and, as she had been taught, stepped back to see how it sat on the page. Normally, the accident in the motorway tunnel would have been the lead story but Greg's scoop was more important and the crash had been relegated to the bottom of the page.

She shuddered as she looked and the mangled, burnt-out wreckage in the picture. Frustratingly, the police had still not released the name of the driver. She had been ringing everyone she knew to try and get a fix on his or her identity but without any results save promises to ring back.

She took a deep breath and clicked to send the newspaper to the printers in Seville. She would pick up the print run at the station in the morning. Then the problems would really begin.

She gathered her things together. She was in the habit of sleeping in the office the night of a print run. It made it easier to pick up the papers early. Just as she was about to turn off the lights the phone rang. The screen showed that it was her friend Juanita at the Guardia office.

"Juanita. I just went to press"

"Sorry Mary. I said I would let you know when we had identified the driver of that motorway crash. The dental searches just arrived. I have a name for you.

The person killed in the car accident was called Scott MacDonald. He used to be a footballer. He had been drinking and taking drugs. Sorry."

Mary felt a cold chill creep up her spine. It couldn't be a coincidence that Scottie had blown the whistle on the goings on at the Mayor's office and is then involved in a fatal accident. Besides he didn't drink.

She peered out of the window. Two men were sitting in a red car in the otherwise empty street. She suddenly felt very alone. She hadn't taken the death threats seriously but Scottie.....

Greg had given her the number of a detective that had asked him some questions. She needed some help urgently.

* * *

Rio settled back to thinking about Anya and what to do with her. Did she want her to move to Madrid so that they could be together? Ever since Rio had been in Malaga Anya had become increasingly needy and in one sense it was wearing thin. On the other hand, she was becoming extremely fond of her.

Her mobile phone interrupted her deliberations. Mary's small frightened voice explained the problem.

"Stay where you are. I am five minutes away."

The bar was a couple of blocks away from the Enquirer's offices. Rio drew her gun deliberately as she strode down the street to the office. Initially, the car stayed where it was but as she came nearer it sped off narrowly missing her. She identified Huertas as the driver.

Mary buzzed her into the office. She had been watching from the window.

"You chased them away," she said gratefully "I was scared that they might force their way in."

"Very likely," said Rio as she checked out the office "but you should be safe enough with me here.

Is your husband still in the hospital?"

"Yes, but he has a police guard. After what happened to Scottie he needs it more than ever"

Rio sat her down "What happened to Scottie?"

"Sorry I assumed that you knew. My contact in the local police rang me when they got the results of the dental tests back. It was Scottie who was killed in that dreadful accident on the motorway.

They said that he had been drinking and taking drugs but he never touched alcohol and was very against using drugs. When he was playing he even fronted one of those films that try to put youngsters off."

"You think that someone killed him"

"He was exposing Mayor Mijas. Isn't it obvious?"

"I would prefer to have some evidence before we start jumping to conclusions. Just because a couple of the Mayor's hoodlums were watching the office doesn't necessarily make them homicidal. When you say he was exposing the Mayor, what do you mean."

"It is all over the front page of tomorrow's Enquirer. Scottie hacked into the system at the municipal centre and found all the evidence." Mary turned pale "Oh my God. Inez. I must ring her."

"Inez is safe. She is staying with friends. Someone wrecked their apartment" Rio decided not to mention the memory stick.

Mary shook her head. "There have been loads of threats but nothing physical until this. We really must have hit the bullseye. Tomorrow everyone will know."

"We'll deal with that tomorrow. Firstly, we need to find you somewhere safe to stay, secondly, I need to call for some reinforcements."

"I am going to sleep here. I sent the paper to be printed overnight and in the morning I'll take Bessie down to the station and pick up the local copies for distribution."

"I think it would be far better if we moved you to a safe house – preferably outside the area where the Mijas name has less clout."

"I have to deal with the paper, otherwise it has all been in vain. Greg's injuries, Scottie's death..." she choked on the words. "I just have to."

Rio knew when to give in. "OK as you wish – but once you have dealt with it we will move you. What time do you start in the morning?"

She looked crestfallen "You are not leaving? I would feel much safer if you stayed with me."

Rio looked her over. Quite attractive, mid-thirties maybe older. Straight but maybe curious. Important witness in the case. Off-limits for sure.

"Of course," she said "I will camp down over here. You get some sleep."

When she rang it sounded as though Toro was in a bar.

"Sorry to disturb you but I need some assistance."

She told him the story and as ever, Toro was quick to anger "Bastards" he said "Is that this little runt Huertas? I should have dealt with him when we had them at the station.

I will drive down tonight. If I grab a few hours' sleep I'll set out around two and meet you at the Enquirer office at seven o'clock."

"Can you tell Baltasar and the Judge"

"No problem. By the way, those files look dynamite. I only glanced through them before they went off to the experts but if they show what I think they show Mijas is history."

Rio settled down on her makeshift bed of office chairs. As she drifted off she was wondering how she was going to explain to Anya how she spent the night with another woman.

Protocol

Davies had been clear "If you are summoned upstairs it will be some load of bollocks that they can't be arsed to come down here for but if they do come down to see you, you can bet your life that the shit has, is hitting or is about to hit the fan."

Amanda Smallbone shut the door of Butler's office – not , according to Davies, a good sign. Rather than sit she paced slowly around the office. "I have just had an interesting phone call," she said, "it seems your enquiries have hit a sore spot."

Mentally, Butler sorted through the large list of cases regarded as in progress for a clue. "Good," he said encouragingly "That must mean we are getting somewhere."

"The phone call was a complaint, albeit an unofficial one, that you have not been following procedures laid down by the United Nations and endorsed by the European Council."

"So we are talking Interpol or Europol – and are they are upset?"

"Not as far as I know – but they might become upset at which point we should all be trembling in our boots." Smallbone sat down opposite Butler.

"As I am sure you will become aware if you haven't been told already, I used to be responsible for international liaison before I was promoted.

I enjoyed it – the jollies particularly – amongst which was a conference on cross-border policing in Aarhus. At this conference, I met a Spanish judge by the name of Hector Diamante.

After a lot of Danish beer, topped off with Spanish wine I made the mistake of letting him get too close."

Butler smiled "I get the picture"

"Anyway, despite my balanced and proportionate use of unarmed combat skills learned courtesy of the British taxpayer to deter his advances, this Spanish arsehole regards me as some kind of friend with whom he can share any and every problem that arises when the Spanish and British police forces talk to each other."

"The phone call was from the arsehole"

"It was. You have been asking questions about a Spanish citizen – a Mr Mijas – without invoking the necessary protocols."

Butler raised an eyebrow. "I have?"

"You have. Consider yourself admonished. The question is did you get anything useful?"

"Some interesting local colour but the main focus of our unofficial enquiry was, in fact, Derek Sanderson. Mijas was only mentioned because they met."

"Who is Mijas?"

"A significant Spanish criminal it is believed."

"By whom?"

"My contact – Judge Rojo"

Smallbone sat back in the chair "Now it begins to make sense"

"Do you know Jesus Rojo?"

"I know of him and where his responsibilities lie. Now I understand why Diamante would be so exercised about your questions."

Butler opened the file. "Derek Sanderson is suspected of funding the Brighton scam."

Smallbone shrugged "I know the name but I can't think from where."

"He runs a large asset management company in the West End and has a big house up in Sussex. His background is in finance and the NCA has been interested in his activities for some time. Rojo was also looking to identify him after he and Mijas were seen together."

Smallbone was up and pacing again "Judge Rojo is responsible for the fight against corruption – important, high-level stuff." She turned and looked directly at Butler "Serious political stuff and all that that entails. Is this Mijas a public official?"

"A city mayor"

"So we have evidence that connects a senior Spanish judge, a British financier and a local Mayor with what exactly?"

"According to Rojo, he has been selling construction permits to developers."

"And why does that affect us?"

"Honestly? We are not sure yet. Sanderson's company has fingers in a lot of pies including the company in Brighton selling Spanish villas. So, if Rojo is right, he may well be the money behind the developers buying the hooky planning permissions from Mijas."

* * *

A phone call from the General Council was always a sign that someone was concerned that an investigation was impinging upon someone else's territory or perhaps getting too close for comfort.

Rojo had taken the call in his office and shut the door which was another sign of its importance. After a while, Baltasar watched as he placed the receiver very deliberately on the phone then gave it the finger.

"Whose lawn do we have our tanks on now?" he asked cheerily.

Rojo smiled grimly. "Diamante is causing trouble with the General Council. He is complaining that I tried to entrap him when all he was doing was giving me advice."

"I thought you were buying him lunch"

"So did I, but things got a little heated when he saw Toro recording our conversation."

"So what?"

"Indeed. So what? Judge Campo was just warning me of the complaint unofficially. He dislikes Diamante as much as anyone else, but he has to go through the motions. I reminded him that, technically, we abide by their rules only out of courtesy."

"That gives him the perfect excuse to tell Diamante where to put his complaint."

"Yes, but he is clever enough to know that the best course is to kick it into the long grass and just let the complaint run out of steam. Unless someone is pushing an agenda, these things take years. Anyway, we can discuss it with the learned judge Diamante tomorrow."

"Speaking of complaints did you hear that the locals are complaining about the other night? That little arse wipe Huertas is saying that Rio ran him off the road into that slurry pit and assaulted him before he was arrested."

Rojo laughed "Assaulted him? He doesn't know Rio. If she had assaulted him he would still be feeling the bruises."

"He has instructed some tin-pot local lawyer to put together a formal complaint. The local force should have just shut it down immediately but for some reason, we are not on their Christmas card list.

I can't believe that it will come to anything but it there will probably have to be interviews which will be a bloody nuisance."

"I admire their nerve. Looking through the history of these complaints they have been running for years.

The local investigators have had numerous opportunities to bring the corruption to a conclusion but they have fluffed every chance. Now they choose to stick their necks out over a trivial complaint."

"Anyone would think that they are protecting Mijas" Baltasar was becoming angry "It reflects badly on all of us when this happens and makes our pursuit of the real criminals all the harder.

Now we have to waste time and resources defending trumped-up charges because they can't be bothered to do their job properly."

"So be it" Rojo shrugged "We can drag it out until this case is resolved then it too will run into the sand."

* * *

When Amanda Smallbone was worried a small tic became apparent beside her left eye.

"I assume, from what you say, that we have very little in terms of actual evidence that Sanderson is involved in criminal activity at all, let alone in our jurisdiction."

"Not so far" Butler nodded "Although he has a file an inch thick, it is difficult to see why he would be involved in a grubby little deposit-taking scam.

However, once you add in development to the picture it starts to make more sense if the forward sales are used to fund the development.

Sanderson is known to Fraud, Financial crime, the NCA and, interestingly, to Sergeant Davies."

She smiled "Our very own criminal encyclopaedia."

"They tried to interrogate him about a currency fraud but someone high up put a stop to it."

Smallbone leaned forward conspiratorially. "I have remembered where I have seen the name Sanderson.

He is a contact associated with Proudfoot – captain of his local golf club I believe. There have been several interventions involving Sanderson or members of his family that are being investigated – but not by you.

Keep that information firmly under your hat. If you come across anything involving Proudfoot in your investigations bring it straight to me."

"Understood"

"What about the guy running the Brighton operation? Fisher was it?"

"He is in our sights. I plan to bring him in and lean on him. He may well be our best opportunity to link Sanderson to the operation. They must have been in contact."

"Don't leave it too long. I appreciate that you are trying to give him enough rope and so on but from a local perspective we need to start showing some results.

The statistics don't discriminate between the arrest of a little slag like Fisher and the apprehension of a criminal mastermind."

"I am sure the NCA will give credit where it is deserved."

Smallbone snorted "Setting aside the fact that they wouldn't give us the drippings from the end of their nose unless they were forced to, credit is useless.

What counts are the number of arrests set against the number of reported crimes."

"We will feel his collar soon enough."

"Glad to hear it. While I am happy that we help out our Spanish friends as much as possible, please remember that we are working under significant budgetary constraints.

Personally, I don't give a rats arse whether you are sticking to protocol or not but I will care a lot if you overspend my budget particularly without nailing a significant criminal over here even though you are just going to bugger off back to the NCA when it is over."

Butler bit back "Understood – but if he is funding bad things in Spain – he has likely been naughty closer to home."

"Then we had better find out how naughty." Smallbone opened the door to leave. "You might need some specialist help to unravel accounts and so on. I will see what I can do.

By the way, don't feel any pressing need to talk to God about this. What I said about protocol? He does care. Best if he plays golf with an easy conscience."

Large calibre

Hector Diamante was a proud man. Proud of his position as a senior judge. Proud of his achievements. Proud of his house, his wife, his children, his cars and his mistress. Two days before, when he saw that Jesus Rojo had made an appointment to see him, he knew instinctively that it was all over.

Sitting at his desk he allowed self-righteous anger to wash over him. He was a well-respected man, an advisor to Government ministers, a *consejuero* to the Council of State – by what right was he being questioned by an upstart like Rojo? He was not even a real Spaniard

"*Chucho Ingles*" he muttered.

Pedigree counted, even in modern Spain, perhaps especially in modern Spain where all sense of class had been washed away by a liberal elite representing Madrid and truly little else.

With a few diversions along the way, Diamante could trace his lineage back to the noble house of Albacete, created by Ferdinand and Isabella in 1492. Who was more worthy of respect? A real Spanish nobleman or an English mongrel?

He scanned the framed certificates on the wall. In pride of place the award from Universidad Autónoma de Madrid that read "*La Mejor mente legal - 1972*" – top of his graduate year.

Those were years full of hope. The dog days of the Franco regime. A new beginning. As a newly qualified lawyer, he had even helped to draft the new constitution. Rojo had no right to question him – no right at all.

Swirling the black pearl cognac around the bowl, he sipped it gently, drawing in the aroma and feeling the warming spirit slip down smoothly. The Maral was leaning against his desk. His favourite brandy, his favourite rifle. If lessons were needed – he was the man to teach them and this was his weapon of choice.

Reaching into his desk drawer he retrieved a silver case and a slender silver tube. A line of the best quality cocaine from an impeccable source - just the thing to steady his hand as he drew a bead on his enemies.

Of course, Rojo would not come alone. It would be too much to expect of his sense of honour that they should sort this out man to man. Last time he brought the tall one – Toro - and he, Hector Diamante, saw through him immediately.

This time he would probably bring Dos Rios - notoriously quick with her fists and her gun. She would undoubtedly shoot first before asking whether the death of her boss was justified or honourable. His own mortality wrapped itself around him like a cloak and he shivered momentarily.

He reached into his jacket pocket and took out his Mont Blanc fountain pen. Opening his diary, he wrote a few words. He blotted them carefully before reaching down and unlacing his right shoe. He slipped off his silk sock and placed it neatly in the shoe next to his desk.

Honour was important. That is what people didn't seem to understand. Everyone was so obsessed with their modern lives, their smartphones, the internet and so on that they had forgotten the basic Spanish virtues of honour and respect.

Respect that was his by right – still, they, - Rojo - would learn.

* * *

148

Baltasar looked up at the imposing white limestone of the Cybele Palace. Diamante did alright for himself.

"Isn't this the City Council?"

Rojo grunted. "I think so. Politicians always get the best space in any city"

"So why is a judge based here"

"Diamante advises the City on legal matters – they keep an office for him in return"

The door was guarded by a young officer from the municipal police. Unusually, a handgun was displayed prominently on his hip.

"Judge Rojo and I are here to see Judge Diamante," Said Baltasar producing his warrant card. The policeman snapped to attention. "Relax." Baltasar murmured. "We don't want to draw attention to ourselves. What is your name?"

Sebastian Lopez was not used to being addressed by superior officers other than in the acceptance of orders. Generally, he got on with his job, did as he was told and kept his head down. Now he was being asked his name by a Chief Inspector from the national force. Every instinct told him that nothing good would come of this.

"Lopez" he stammered, followed by a belated "sir".

"Have you been on duty all morning?" Things were going from bad to worse. Now a judge was asking him questions. He intended to say "Yes, your honour" but his throat merely uttered a strangulated noise.

Rojo smiled. "There is no need to be nervous. I was wondering if you would recognise Judge Diamante?"

149

The smile did nothing to put Lopez at his ease. "I know who he is your honour. He arrived around an hour ago."

The chief inspector resumed the interrogation. "Good. You notice him coming and going from the building. Have you noticed whether he gets any regular visitors?"

Lopez knew that there would be a trick question – and this was it. If he answered no, the response would likely stop the inquisition and allow him to breathe easily again. On the other hand, Chief Inspector Baltasar would think him an idiot lacking basic observational skills. He had observed that the impeccably-dressed Judge Diamante kept company with several people that didn't share his appreciation of a sharp suit.

"Yes Sir. I don't know their names but I know their faces."

"Good. We have some pictures back at our office. We will need you to come down and look at them –soon. This is an ongoing investigation."

Lopez was searching his memory feverishly. Rojo. Judge Rojo. Was he the one responsible for rounding up the drug barons? He knew the name from somewhere.

"Of course, Sir"

The judge patted him lightly on the arm. "Good work Lopez."

A sweeping staircase rose from a very grand lobby. An atrium soared up six floors allowing sunlight to diffuse into the core of the building. Balconies gave a view from each floor.

"Judge Rojo and Chief Inspector Baltasar to see Judge Diamante." The girl at the reception desk glanced through them and produced two passes from a box on her desk.

"If you could wear these please at all times in the building. The lifts are on your right. You need the third floor - Room 207"

The sound of the gunshot echoed around the atrium and time slowed. The receptionist flinched and reached for the alarm. A security guard emerged from his office bemused. A scream wailed from the upper floors.

Balthasar's first instinct was to protect his boss. Pistol in hand he bundled Rojo to the side of the lobby away from the doors. The alarm was sounding and people began to emerge from their offices.

"If I were the target I would already be dead," Rojo muttered as Baltasar gazed up onto the balcony and Lopez burst through the front door gun in hand.

Baltasar intercepted him. "Stay with me and watch our backs."

The wailing got louder as a distraught secretary emerged onto a balcony half-way up the atrium holding her bloodied hands out in front of her, almost in supplication.

"Third floor, now" The security guard barked into his radio and set off followed by Baltasar, Rojo and Lopez.

A crowd of onlookers was milling around in the corridor, uncertain what had happened. Baltasar took immediate control. "Ladies and Gentlemen. This is a health and safety emergency. Can you please move back to your offices and stay inside. Officer Lopez will take each of your names and make arrangements for you to give a statement."

The security guard began to usher the frightened occupants back and away from Diamante's office. Rojo took the secretary gently by the arm and led her back into the scene of the crime and sat her down in the corner.

The desk was largely undisturbed by events. A large, leather-bound diary sat in prime position, its cover defaced by a spattering of blood. An empty brandy glass sat on a slate coaster next to an open fountain pen.

Diamante was still sitting in his chair but it had moved backwards through ninety degrees leaving his feet dangling in mid-air. The left foot was expensively clad in a patent-leather Italian Derby, the other was pale and naked. The matching shoe with a discarded silk sock hanging out of it lay by the desk. The Browning rifle lay between his legs, propped up against the chair as if by design.

Lopez peered at the corpse eyes wide and mouth open. Under Diamante's chin was a blackened area containing a small hole. In the top of the head was a much larger hole and, spread up the wall behind the chair was a large part of the finest legal mind of 1972. Lopez felt sick. He had never seen so much blood.

"Officer Lopez" Baltasar snapped. Lopez stiffened. "Yes Sir" he mumbled. Rojo took his arm.

"Your first body?" Lopez nodded soundlessly. "I sympathise. It is always a shock. There will be time for reflection later. Right now we need your help. Are you OK with that?"

Lopez nodded, still in a daze.

"We need to keep what happened here confidential for a short while. Only the people in this room know what happened. As far as the outside world is concerned the bang was caused by a short circuit that injured the judge and his secretary. Concentrate on taking the names and contact details of everyone on this floor.

We will deal with statements and DNA later. Call your shift commander, tell him that I have drafted you into my team temporarily and to arrange for your immediate replacement. Give him my name but no details. Tell him to contact me if he misunderstands anything."

Lopez shut the door behind him. Diamante's secretary was sitting almost catatonic staring at her hands "We will put her in protective custody for a couple of days to keep her out of circulation." Baltasar nodded "I will arrange for a car and a policewoman to take her to the office."

Rojo sat next to the secretary "I am Judge Rojo. What is your name?" She looked at him blankly then stammered "Dorothea".

"Have you worked for Judge Diamante long Dorothea?" The tears began to flow again and he put his arm around her shoulders. "No" she stuttered "his normal secretary is on holiday for two weeks. The agency sent me to cover for her. This was my first day."

"Some first day. Our priority is your safety, Dorothea. So that we can keep you safe we need to keep you with us for a couple of days. Soon an officer will be coming to take you to our facility in Salamanca. Is there anyone that you need to tell that you will be away?"

"Am I being arrested?"

"No of course not, but we need to protect you. Some very bad men have done this and if they think that you know anything you are at risk."

* * *

Baltasar shook his head. "Why use a cannon like this? It always makes such a mess."

Rojo scanned the papers on Diamante's desk. "He was a hunter. Wild boar I think." As an investigating judge Rojo had been to many crime scenes – far too many of them had involved significant amounts of gore for his liking.

"He could have stopped an elephant with this. I always had him down as a small calibre kind of guy." Baltasar pulled on the rubber gloves kept in his pocket for crime scenes.

Rojo the photographer searched the room methodically, breaking it down into a series of shots. On the wall opposite the desk hung a huge tapestry of one of the Don Quixote tableaux in the Royal Palace. A copy but old nevertheless.

The hardwood filing cabinets with brass fittings on the adjacent wall, the brass lamps and the leather desk furniture all showed Diamante's obsession with tradition over function. The whole office would not have looked out of place in a turn of the century drama.

Through the frosted glass of the window wall outlines and shadows moved as Lopez processed the witnesses to the crime scene.

On the wall behind the desk, the blood was already starting to turn into a black smear.

"The priority is to seal and search the room and its contents. Tell me what you see."

Baltasar raised a seasoned eyebrow. "White male, fifties, dead on inspection. Entry gunshot wound below the chin, exit wound to the back of the head.

Weapon adjacency suggests that the victim inflicted the wound himself."

"No sign of any other hand?"

Baltasar was examining the desk. "Nothing obvious. It looks a classic suicide.

He was sitting at his desk with the rifle between his knees. The recoil caused the chair to fall backwards.

He didn't fancy putting the barrel in his mouth so pressed it under his chin. He was lucky he got the angle right otherwise he would just have blown off half his face. I have seen that happen."

He leaned down to check for a pulse.

"No pulse. Because the rifle is quite long he has pulled the trigger with his toe. Once forensics have had a look at it we will be able to confirm that.

From the size of the exit wound, I would say that he was using a hollow pointed round. Is that typical of boar hunting?"

Rojo shrugged "I have heard it said that it stops the animal more quickly but others try to avoid them because they destroy too much of the shoulder meat."

He bent over the desk. "There are traces of white powder. I imagine that it is cocaine followed by a glass of expensive brandy to give him the balls."

Baltasar lifted the cover of the diary with his pen. "Let's see if he had any interesting visitors." The diary fell open on the current page.

He turned slowly "This was staged for our benefit. He left you a message."

Written in Diamante's cultured hand in capital letters across the page was "Fuck you, Rojo."

Bessie

It was as if the old building was alive, creaking and groaning as it breathed in and out. Rio woke several times during the night, checking the doors each time. Finally, she woke with the sunrise and was surprised by a naked Mary walking into the shower. "I'll be done soon" she shouted over her shoulder "Feel free to use the facilities."

The hot shower helped with her aching back. The gap between the two chairs had been sufficient to cause a spasm through lack of support. Feeling irrationally modest she had waited until Mary had dressed fully before stripping off and stepping under the streaming flow of water. The facilities only extended to Granola with milk so she refused breakfast, opting for just a black americano from the Enquirer machine.

The van was parked outside the back of the building. Rio checked it for obvious signs of tampering but found none. She sat inside while Mary chatted to the porters at the station as they loaded the bales of newspapers into the back. She noticed from her phone that Anya had rung half a dozen times.

"I don't want to hurry you but my colleague is meeting us at your office at seven"

Mary was bright-eyed and keen to get on with her deliveries. The events of the previous evening had been relegated to the back of her mind. "OK," she said, "I'll do the local shop first."

They parked outside the office and she strode off with one of the bales in the direction of the café at the end of the road. Rio could see Toro leaning against a car further down the road. She took one of the papers and ambled off to see him.

"Did any of them show up overnight?" Toro was itching for a fight

Rio smiled "No. I think they got the message but they are going to be mightily pissed when they see this." She showed him the paper.

Toro whistled "That should set the hares running."

"I am worried that retribution might be the first thing on their list."

A red Seat sped past them and stopped next to Bessie. Toro shouted and began to run towards it, drawing his gun as he went. A bottle flew out of the passenger window and rolled under the van. Bessie exploded in a ball of fire as the car drove off at speed.

* * *

By the time the *bombaderos* had finished, the whole area stank of diesel and decay. The interior of the van was almost entirely gone save for the front passenger seat. The whole thing stood in a pool of blackened water and shattered glass where the firefighters had subjected the blaze to a blast of water. The blistered skin had largely peeled off revealing the skeleton beneath but on the passenger door a painted butterfly was visible mourning its missing companions.

A small crowd had begun to form, peering at the blackened shell.

"Bessie" Mary held her blackened hands to her face. "The paper." Rio hugged her maternally. "It was Mijas and his thugs that did this," she said between sobs.

"I am sure of it and you be sure that we will bring them to justice. Just be thankful that you weren't sitting in it when it happened." Toro had crossed the line from angry to furious "I have seen that red Seat before."

"Just because we publish the truth."

Rio wiped Mary's eyes with her handkerchief. "Telling the truth can be painful. Now will you let us find you a safe place?"

She nodded "What about Greg?"

"I am guessing that he is recovered enough to be moved"

Toro intervened "I left Baltasar arranging an ambulance to transfer him to Madrid. You are both in danger."

"How do you want to play this?"

Toro pursed his lips. "I would like to go and find Mr Huertas. I am sure that it was his car – the one that he drove into the shit."

"I think that will have to wait." Rio could see that it was likely to be a bloody encounter. She had seen Toro in action in circumstances like these and it hadn't been pretty. "Can you look after Mary. Take her home to pick up some things. I will go to the hospital to check on the transfer and make sure our man is being looked after. Can you bring her there."

* * *

The policeman was standing outside the main entrance smoking when Rio arrived. He nodded, recognising her.

"How is Mister Matthews doing," she asked.

"The journalist? I don't know. We have been reassigned. Other priorities. I just heard."

"So there is no-one with him?"

"Some doctor just arrived to see him just as I left."

Rio sprinted into the hospital and into the corridor where the policeman should have been sitting. As she neared the room she could see a man in a white coat bearing a syringe. She recognised Caballo immediately.

The first kick ruptured the collateral ligament at the side of Caballo's knee causing him to fall away from Matthews. The second hit him in the right armpit, dislocating his shoulder. The full syringe clattered to the floor as he screamed in pain. Rio could see the gun in a shoulder holster as he tried to grab it with his good hand. "No. No. No." she said, wagging her forefinger, and watched as his hand returned to the floor. "Inspector Toro sends his regards," she said stamping on his left hand, breaking two fingers. Matthews was staring at her wide-eyed.

"Are you OK?"

He nodded. "I am now"

The doctor accompanied by two burly porters arrived in response to Caballo's screams. He nodded an acknowledgement.

"You were here the other day. What the fuck is going on? I will not have fighting in my hospital. This man needs help."

Rio smiled courteously. "A policeman is standing outside the main entrance. Could you fetch him. I need him to make an arrest before you assist him with his injuries."

The doctor nodded curtly and one of the porters ran off.

"He is badly injured. What are you charging him with?"

"Attempted murder will do for starters," said Rio retrieving the syringe from the floor. "He was attempting to inject your patient with this."

The doctor looked incredulously at the label.

"but this is insulin. In this dose it would kill."

"My point exactly"

* * *

The policeman had been shocked at the state of the whimpering Caballo and called immediately for backup. He was starting to push back on Rio's request that he be arrested when the reassuring bulk of Toro appeared in the doorway.

"Mary is in the car. What is the status of the ambulance?"

"My patient isn't going anywhere" the doctor spat angrily. "I cancelled the ambulance that was due to take him to Madrid. He will be well enough to be discharged tomorrow anyway. I am not going to waste my budget ferrying him around the country."

Toro looked from the Doctor to Caballo then to Matthews. "Can you walk?" he asked.

"I am a bit shaky I'm afraid," said Matthews.

He pointed at Caballo. "Is he arrested?" The policeman shook his head in response.

"Inspector Dos Rios has asked you nicely to arrest this piece of dirt but you have not done so. Now Inspector Toro of the CNP is giving you a direct order to arrest him."

"I am waiting for orders" squeaked the policeman

"Are you deaf? I just gave you an order. Do it now" he roared and scooping Matthews up from the bed he turned to leave.

161

For a moment the Doctor considered blocking the doorway but noticed that the porters had melted back into the corridor.

"Just deal with your other patients." Said Toro "I have this one under control."

* * *

It was clear that Mary had become persona non grata amongst the local community. The concierge at her apartment made a point of spitting on the floor as they approached and muttered *bajo* as they walked past. Toro hadn't understood, until Mary told him, that the majority of readers of the paper did so online so burning the paper copies had been fruitless.

As they left the apartment an earnest-looking lady with grey hair laid into Mary verbally, accusing her of dishonouring the Mayor and the country by making up stories. "Go home" she had shouted as they drove off.

"I think it is safe to say that they don't believe everything they read in the papers" observed Mary.

Toro made Greg Matthews as comfortable as possible in the back seat and Mary climbed in to comfort him. He was looking for Rio when a squad car with siren blaring pulled up outside the hospital entrance and three officers climbed out. He noticed with amusement as Rio held open the door for them as they ran into the building.

"We are off to Madrid" he shouted "Good luck with the locals"

Rio waved. Her main concern at the moment was one particular local who had rung again while she was in the hospital.

The key

She raised her head to look at the clock for what seemed like the millionth time. After prescribing an early night she had tossed and turned, seeing every hour pass. She had declined Mickey's offer of a couple of days in Bristol but she always slept badly when he was away.

Even when she did sleep the dream conspired to wake her. She was in the dock and family after family were testifying about how she had cheated them out of their life savings.

There was no doubt in her mind that she was guilty on all counts.

In the cool light of the morning, she began to take stock of all the things she knew about Mickey's venture.

As far as she knew he hadn't held anything back from her. She knew that the base idea was to take money from families wanting to buy property in Spain based on a lie; she knew that the idea was funded by someone else - she needed to find out who.

Mickey's desk was in the spare bedroom. She tried each of the drawers in turn. One was devoted to his car, his pride and joy. She had a flashback to the day he had picked it up from the garage. She had never seen him so happy. They went for a drive along the coast and ended up in a hotel in Rye.

She sat in the office chair. They had talked about going to Australia or South Africa to live one of these days. She had always fancied the south of France but Mickey couldn't hack the language barrier.

She knew that it stemmed from his suspicious nature - he wouldn't be able to understand whether or not they were putting one over on him. Since he spent his life trying to gain an advantage over others she saw his point.

When she raised the question of her mother he had remained silent.

Although she had loved Mickey, she was under no illusion. She just knew that when the circumstance arose and he had to leave, he would do so alone.

She would be left to fend for herself and her mother. In those circumstances, she needed to know as much as she could to give herself leverage. She carried on with her search.

The next drawer she tried was full of office paraphernalia - staples, paperclips, adhesive tape, a few pens and a notebook. Unless it was written in code, the notebook revealed little, just a few doodles.

The top drawer was locked. She scanned the desk for keys but her attention was caught by a card propped up against the side of the computer screen. It was an invitation to an event at Sutton House near Midhurst on the previous Wednesday.

She remembered him going. She had asked him what it was about and he had said that he was "meeting the money." She examined the card in more detail.

It appeared to be from someone called Jasmine Oh who was writing on behalf of the team at Reichenbach inviting "Mister Fisher" to an afternoon of entertainment and networking at Sutton House. No mention of money.

She began to search through the bookcase systematically, taking out each volume and shaking it to see if anything had been hidden amongst the pages.

After the first shelf she had discovered a fifty-pound note - obviously some kind of emergency money - and a fifth of Scotch hidden in the complete works of William Shakespeare.

She remembered him getting it as a birthday present from his workmates back when he had a proper job. That was back in the day when she thought he could do no wrong - then he was sacked over a misunderstanding involving expenses.

Through the window she saw the Jaguar pull up. Quickly she shut the desk drawers and rearranged the papers on his desk tucking the invitation in the back pocket of her jeans.

"You would never make a burglar" he laughed as he opened the front door "I could see you as plain as day"

"I was looking for some sticky tape" she lied, gave him a welcome kiss, and realised that breaking their bond would be as easy as that.

"How did you get on in Bristol?"

Mickey shrugged "OK I suppose. I spoke to several agents. Unloaded three boxes of brochures. I was too knackered to eat out so I just got room service to knock me up some pasta.

All pretty uneventful really."

"What was the hotel like?"

"Typical city centre business hotel. Room too hot, too small, dominated by the TV with a brochure touting their mucky films. You know the type."

"I didn't miss anything then?"

He smiled "Ah. Had you come along I was going to suggest that we stay further out. There is this little converted mill I know that has a large bath en-suite to every room. Baths big enough for two." He drew her to him and kissed her softly.

She felt her resolve beginning to melt then as soon as it came the moment was lost.

"I fancy a Thai this evening" he whispered in her ear "Shall I make us a reservation?"

She pushed him away "You think of nothing but your stomach."

"That's a yes then" he laughed "I have to pop by the office. I'll pick you up about seven." And with that he was gone.

She watched as he climbed into the Jaguar then, as it sped away, she returned to his office to continue her search.

Sometime later she sat down to take stock. The contents of the locked drawer had been a disappointment. She found the key on the windowsill, hidden in plain sight. There were more bits and pieces – a couple of clean memory sticks and another notebook.

This only had one page with anything on it. It was headed *SPAIN*, underlined and consisted of a series of initials with numbers after them.

Interestingly MF had 500 against his name but SF, presumably Sharon Fellows, only had 25. So much for being an equal partner.

Perhaps she was misjudging him – there was no evidence that she could find of any other women, nor of any criminal activity.

She was about to close the drawer when she noticed something had been caught at the back. With difficulty she freed an estate agent's key fob. On one side it showed the agents name – Maugham and Frost - on the other it said, simply, Wellington Road.

Sharon's first thought was another woman. She knew Mickey had had a reputation for playing away when they first got together but he had insisted that it was all behind him.

A scenario began to form in her mind of him taking the tart to Bristol with him but she banished it from her mind.

Where was Wellington Road? According to the computer, there were dozens of them, including, she noted, one in Bristol. She knew Maugham and Frost had an office in the city centre. If it was a local agent, then surely it would be within their area.

"Maugham and Frost, how may I help?"

"I have found one of your keys." She told herself that it wasn't a lie - she didn't need to say where she found it.

"Thank you for letting us know. As you can imagine this is always happening. Could you tell me the serial number of the key so that I can contact the tenant?"

Sharon read out the series of tiny numbers engraved on the key.

"Thank you. I will let Mr Fisher know that you have found his key. Can I have your name and address so we can pick it up?"

"Mr Fisher? Mickey Fisher?"

"That's right"

"I know him. I need to talk to him about something. I can drop it off"

167

"Even better"

"What number Wellington Road is it?"

"Number seven. If you are going down there any time soon I should warn you that the centre of the city is gridlocked and the traffic is being diverted around Hove."

"Thanks," said Sharon "I will make sure he gets it back. Oh, have you got the postcode for my satnav?"

An extra pair of hands

The early morning sun blasted through the windows at the end of the office turning Rojo into a silhouette as he walked into the office, coffee in hand. He took in the scene. Several empty desks, a screen where notes, pictures and seemingly random ideas were pinned. Baltasar was hunched over a keyboard. He had never quite mastered touch-typing despite his many years of practice.

"How is he getting on?" Baltasar peered across the office to the glass booth. Lopez was looking intently at a screen comparing the case pictures.

"He seems to be quite sharp. So far he has identified Parador and the two heavies we arrested but not Mijas."

Rojo made a face. "A pity. I guess you wouldn't expect him to come to Madrid when he is calling the shots down south. What about the Englishman?"

"No. Nothing. I am guessing he only really deals with Mijas."

"What do you think of Lopez?"

Baltasar smiled. "I remember my first body. Oddly enough that was another suicide. He had thrown himself under a train at Delicias – the old one. The train had cut him in half. I spent the first half-hour of the investigation throwing up. Lopez appears to be made of stronger stuff."

"He was very efficient at Diamante's office. We have a complete dataset of witnesses and their details notated with what he knows about each potential witness. If you like him and I like him..."

"That just leaves Toro"

"He will be back soon. I will put Lopez with him. He needs to go down to the hospital and put the squeeze on the journalist. If they get on I will arrange for him to be seconded on a more permanent basis."

"I had his commander on the phone just now whining about a lack of manpower. I told him that Lopez needed time off for counselling after the shock of the suicide. I don't think he was convinced."

"Toy soldiers" snorted Baltasar contemptuously "They spend all their time wasting people like Lopez on traffic management and crime prevention while people like Mijas run rings around them. If he is any good he needs to transfer to the CNP or the Guardia."

"We can arrange that but let's not get ahead of ourselves. He looks like he will provide the extra pair of hands that we desperately need."

The imposing figure of Toro loomed into view brandishing a file. "I have some preliminary forensics on the dead Judge."

Rojo took the file "anything interesting?"

"He was as high as a kite. No doubt that he shot himself.

Lots and lots of prints in the office that will take time to run through the computer."

"We need you to go down to the hospital and talk to Mr Matthews. We need to know what he knows particularly about Parador, the Planning guy.

He is important, if he is the weak link, when he knows about Diamante, he will be a very scared man."

Toro nodded "How hard do you want me to lean on him? These journos can be a bit precious"

"You need to be gentle with him. After all, if you hadn't intervened, things could have been a lot worse for him. Try to gain his confidence. "

Toro rose to exit. "By the way, can you take Officer Lopez with you. We would rather like your opinion as to whether he might be a useful addition to the team."

"Officer who?"

The thought of a new partner alarmed Toro. Partners needed to be bedded in over a long period. That way they could bond more effectively and learn to trust each other.

"Lopez. He is looking through the pictures"

* * *

It was only a few kilometres from the Salamanca office to the hospital, but the traffic was dreadful. El Clasico was being played that evening at the Bernabéu and the roads were choked with rival fans all determined to see their team win and celebrate accordingly.

Toro hated waiting, whether it was in a supermarket, at a train station or, particularly, in traffic. What he needed, he often thought, was a button that he could press that would turn a set of traffic lights in his favour. Surely that was not beyond the capabilities of Spanish engineers.

He slapped his hands against the steering wheel in frustration.

"So Lopez. You used to direct traffic. How do we get to the hospital quickly?"

Lopez lit up. Much of the past twenty-four hours had passed by in a haze punctuated by brief periods of activity. Collecting the office contacts had allowed him to take his mind of the dreadful scene in the Judge's office but in idle moments he found the image of the dead body persisted.

This was his area of expertise. His special subject.

"Most of the main roads in the centre are part of the new signalling system which is lucky. It means that I can create a clearway through."

He produced his mobile phone and began tapping the screen. "University hospital?"

Toro grunted – traffic policemen had never impressed him. Usually they were creating congestion – not clearing it.

"OK. I have created a clearway from Velasquez to San Bernardo.

As we approach each junction, the opposing lights should turn red and ours should stay green."

As Toro accelerated towards the junction by the Serrano metro station the lights turned green and again as he approached Colon. A broad smile lit up his face.

"I like you, Lopez. You will bring a great deal to the team."

* * *

The policeman snapped to attention as Toro strode up to the secure wing showing his warrant card. Lopez scurried along behind him barely able to keep up.

They found Matthews sitting in a chair beside his bed.

"Mr Matthews. How are you feeling?"

Matthews winced as Toro grasped his hand and pumped his arm. "I am getting better – or so they say. I should be out of here in a couple of days."

"I wouldn't be in too much of a hurry if I were you. There are still some people around who might like to see you suffer a relapse."

"What about my wife? "

"Mary is under our protection until we have resolved this matter. I have some bad news about your van, however. Lopez will fill you in."

Matthews listened as Lopez read out the damage report.

"That van had been with us ever since we came to Spain six years ago" he sighed.

Toro was anxious to move on. "I am sure that there will be compensation both from the insurance company and the criminal scheme. We do need your help in bringing the perpetrators to justice, however."

Matthews felt his ribs tenderly. "Yes. How can I help?"

"The article published by your newspaper contained some extraordinary allegations about several high ranking officials. This is likely connected to the incident with your van. Do you have any actual evidence of the corruption that you write about?"

Matthews shrugged and immediately regretted it. "That depends what you call evidence" He winced. "For years there were rumours about Mijas being paid commissions by several local developers. He was head of town planning before he was elected mayor.

For about five years, his friends won all the regional contracts under his control and developers outside his circle either folded or moved out. That is all fully documented and, according to the civil court, the contracts were all won fair and square in competitive bidding under EU rules."

"I know the case" Lopez said. "The prosecution case was based around the fact that the developers had been given access to privileged information before submitting their final bids – but it was never proved."

Toro looked at him with amazement. "I studied the case at University....." he continued " Civil law. It is quite famous. The Judge dismissed the case because a key witness changed their story."

Matthews continued. "What is not documented is the relationship between Mijas and the developers. It is quite difficult to track.

Mijas controls an account in the name of his wife's company. He isn't named anywhere but all of the friendly developers have used his wife's company to provide what are referred to in the accounts as management services.

They have paid over several million euros amongst them in fees. This is a disproportionately large sum for managing a development. Although it is likely to be used to pay Mijas a substantial pension every month."

Toro pondered what Matthews was saying. "so the files that Scott MacDonald copied are the only things that tie Mijas directly to this." Matthews nodded.

"However compelling this sort of evidence may seem to be, it will take a forensic accounting team to comb through it to uncover anything criminal. Is there anything else? What about Aguilera?"

Matthews paused to drink some water causing himself further discomfort. "Aguilera is something different. For a start, it is a much bigger scheme. With Aguilera, corruption has moved into the planning process itself.

The site is within the national park boundary – so should be undevelopable without what they call a special economic interest statement.

This was intended as a backstop so that they could quarry stone locally and so on. On Mijas say so the planning department has issued a certificate for Aguilera which, as you know, is mainly residential – at least initially."

"Was the certificate challenged by the Regional government?" Lopez was enjoying himself.

"Yes and by the Ministry, but subsidiarity meant that the local view prevailed."

"What a strange decision. I can't think of any case law that would support it."

"The Ministry delegated the decision to an expert Judge to avoid a full-blown hearing."

Toro saw where this was going "Hector Diamante?"

The bloody image of the Judge with half his head missing flooded back to the forefront of Lopez' mind.

Matthews nodded. "There are some other things that are not right with the Aguilera development. The developers, Estados, are not one of Mijas usual crowd. They are foreign-owned.

I thought it might be linked to the mafia but on the face of it, they come from the UK.

The other thing is that nothing much is happening on site. I have been observing the development of property in this area for five years now.

Usually, by the time the name hits the press, the apartments are coming out of the ground. If you go to the Aguilera site there is a portable marketing suite and little else. I think..."

"Hector Diamante is dead."

The statement stopped Matthews in mid-sentence.

"Lopez here attended the scene of his suicide yesterday"

Matthews was taken aback. "Diamante is dead?"

"He blew his head off in his office just as Judge Rojo arrived to interview him"

Lopez felt sick to his stomach.

"He must have realised the game was up. Have the papers covered it?"

"We are sitting on it for a few days. It will be public knowledge next week."

Matthews struggled to his feet. "Can you help me find my clothes. I need to get to the office"

Toro shook his head. "We would rather you didn't report it just yet."

Matthews fell back into his chair "That is all I need. Police censorship."

"Not really. If the political cover for what Mijas and Co are doing has disappeared, we stand a particularly good chance of rolling up the entire network.

If they realised that he had incriminated himself by committing suicide it might spook them into shutting down before we have that chance. We have spoken to your wife. She has agreed to co-operate."

Lopez regained his composure. "Can we talk about the other players in this drama? The mayor, Mijas, has been the focus of your attention. Who else?"

Matthews sighed. "Is there any chance I can have an exclusive on this?"

"That is for Judge Rojo to decide - but let us proceed on that assumption."

"All the documentation has to be authorised by Parador, the head of planning. He knows everything. He is also a man with an expensive lifestyle. He has a trophy wife but also a weakness for young men.

A guy called Raoul tried to sell Mary his story just last week. He showed her some pictures which made her blush to her roots. She has his contact details."

* * *

The two officers sat silently in Toro's car, mentally assessing the story they had been told.

Eventually, Lopez took out his phone. "Should I clear the way back to the office?"

Toro shook his head. "I need time to absorb all this shit. I don't know what makes me angrier - that Spanish public officials should behave this way or that we have been unable to stop them doing it."

"Should I clear the way to a bar?"

Toro smiled. "That is the best suggestion you have made all day. On the way you can tell me all about the Civil Law at University stuff."

Money

"So – Trizer 77 – what do we know?" Butler stood at the whiteboard holding a marker.

"We know we don't like uppity Spanish judges telling us our business" Davies was still sulking over the airport meeting.

"Since it seems that we were not even on the same pitch, it is lucky that his team, who, I would remind you, are on our side, had possession of the ball. Charlie – you have been doing some digging?"

Charlie Finn stood up nervously and cleared her throat "Thanks....boss"

Butler moved on the long pause that followed. "Sorry. This is DS Charlene Finn from the fraud squad who has agreed to help us through this maze. I thought we needed some more technical expertise. Charlie?"

This time she had regained her confidence and began to read from the sheaf of papers clasped in her left hand. "Trizer 77 is an off the shelf company formed and registered in George Town in May 2005. It was number seventy-seven of a batch of registrations undertaken by Fallows and Moore who are locally-based lawyers."

She looked up from the papers catching Davies cynical sneer.

"This is a perfectly normal practice. They are then able to make these shell companies available to their clients."

"What about the directors?"

"Not information on that is available I am afraid."

"What about Fallows and Moore?" Charlene nodded.

"Confidentiality is their reason for existing. It is unlikely that any enquiries of them will be fruitful"

"Who are their clients?"

"A huge list, mostly American but, interestingly, they include Reichenbach Fund Management"

"That may be the link" Butler noted.

"We have done more digging about Reichenbach. Through Europol we have a bit more information about their banking arrangements. The Gibraltar account identified is mainly just a post-box. Most of the money passes through to further accounts in the Cayman Islands and beyond before it disappears. However, some of the money goes elsewhere."

"Anything in Spain?"

"Unfortunately no. Significant sums do go to Switzerland though."

Davies looked blank. "If they don't send money to Spain, how do they buy stuff in Spain?"

"Through their capital accounts. That is all in the public domain. The Gibraltar account isn't."

Butler pursed his lips. "So this is a dead-end?"

"Not necessarily. Cayman used to be a blank wall but it has opened up a lot recently. I have made enquiries but it may take some time and there are no guarantees."

"Do we know if Sanderson has been travelling to these places? Some of you have mates in Borders, see what they can sniff out.

Charlie thanks for this. Would it be possible for you to have a look at Derek Sanderson's finances as well as the Reichenbach stuff?

Davies, time for you and me to start putting a bit of pressure on them."

"I pulled together everything I could find on Reichenbach on the net." Finn handed Butler a memory stick. "Remember that this is all stuff that they want us to see. I was looking for anything hostile to them in the press but they do seem to be all-round good guys with no current enemies that I could find."

"You mean there is some history?"

"Yes. Ten years or so ago they were regarded as a basket case. A bastion of old-world values. The CEO before Sanderson was accused of insider trading and was sent down for it."

"Then Sanderson took over"

"Yes. He cleaned out the stables, invested a lot of money in systems and processes to make them squeaky clean. Part of that was a media strategy to paint them in the best possible light."

* * *

Rojo watched as Lopez grew into the role. As part of his training, he had spent time with the forensic accountancy team and knew his way around a set of accounts as a result.

"There are lots of files on this memory stick. Most of them are pictures of accounts or spreadsheets for different companies all of which appear to be controlled by Juan Mijas."

He displayed several examples on the screen. "Many of them relate to the football club and various transfer fees for players. It is easy to see why Scott MacDonald would be interested in

181

these. They appear to show him being bought not by the football club but by a company called Juvenal. Juvenal owned MacDonald's contract throughout and therefore took the loss when he stopped playing. They also benefitted from the insurance that paid out when he was injured. As I understand it this is an illegal transaction as far as La Liga rules are concerned."

Baltasar was losing patience "Interesting though this is, we are not concerned about how Mijas manages the finances of the football club. What about property development?"

Lopez looked hurt "But it does give an insight into how the man works. The fact that he controls Juvenal, for example, is not in the public domain and not among the interests that he had to declare when elected Mayor. As far as his property interests are concerned these are perhaps the most important files."

The screen showed a credit transaction from a company called Trizer into the Juvenal account for four and a half million euros. It had been notated *Finder's Fee*. A second slide showed an agreement between Trizer and Juvenal that appeared to give Juvenal fifteen per cent of the end value of the Aguilera development.

"The maths here just don't add up," said Lopez "I have done some digging. The Aguilera site would be worth less than a million Euros unless it had a building permit – in which case the value is twenty times that. Surely this Trizer wouldn't be paying this level of fee without knowing that it came with a building permit."

Rojo stood and looked closely at the screen as if trying to identify any flaws. "Look at the date – a full six months before the permits were granted. I can feel him within our grasp" he said, "If we can prove that Mijas controls Juvenal then we have him."

The next slide showed the entry for Juvenal in the Registro Mercantil. It showed Alana Cantaro as the sole Director. Someone had written *Mijas wife* in the margin.

* * *

"I think we have our man but the evidence linking him to Mister Sanderson is at best circumstantial. Certainly, in Spain, I would have a hard time convincing a prosecutor." Rojo and Butler had agreed to talk once they had had a chance to assess the evidence.

Butler agreed "We have little so far but we are working towards a charge of conspiracy to defraud, maybe involving your man. At the very least we should be able to go with joint enterprise charges."

"Mijas is crucial. Soon we will have Senor Parador in custody also. He is a far weaker character and we can use him to unlock the Mayor. Now that Judge Diamante is out of the picture I suspect that, in the end, it will come down to some kind of plea bargain in which case I will ensure that Sanderson is part of the deal."

"They seem to have covered their tracks pretty well"

"Indeed, but I have often found it to be the case that these arrogant, powerful men don't keep their enemies close enough – and it is always their undoing. Mijas has no respect for the force of law. He is used to manipulating the local police force just as he does the local politicians. Because he has no respect he doesn't believe that we will catch him."

"I fear that Sanderson is cut from a different cloth. The law is one dimensional, a thing is either right or it is wrong and we tend to treat cases as a game of chess between good and evil. He is used to analysing complex sets of scenarios and picking the most lucrative course. We are just another set of risk factors in a multi-dimensional universe as far as he is concerned."

"I know a little about chess. I once watched the great Michinsky play his arch-enemy, Zukhov. It was a battle of minds and evenly matched until Zukhov made a mistake by attacking with his bishop when a simple pawn defence would have sufficed. It was a schoolboy error and it cost him the match and ultimately his life. He couldn't take the disgrace and killed himself shortly afterwards. The lesson I learned from that is that it doesn't matter how clever you are, it only takes you to make one mistake and you are lost. From now on we are all looking for Mister Sanderson's mistake."

Once they had said their goodbyes Butler reflected on their conversation. It looked as though Rojo had the Spanish operation tied up and would begin rolling it up. They needed to start on the same path themselves although it looked as though their primary target, Sanderson, would be outside the net when it was hauled in.

He hated being reliant on the Spanish, but a successful arrest would need one of the Spanish suspects to implicate him. Rojo was right, a deal would appear to be the most likely outcome and, if Rojo kept his word, that deal would deliver Derek Sanderson.

Sanderson

"I'll bet this is expensive" The taxi had drawn up outside a large terrace of houses just behind St James Square and Davies was in awe.

"Just remember that they make more money than you or I could dream of, just by picking and choosing where to invest."

"Can I help you, sir?" The uniformed doorman was the keeper of the gate - and knew it. The tone was at once obsequious and threatening.

"Detective Inspector Butler and Detective Sergeant Davies to see Mister Derek Sanderson." Butler noticed that Davies had drawn himself up to his full height and was locked on to the commissionaire. "We have an appointment."

For a moment Butler thought they were going to be barred from entry but he smiled grimly "This way please gentlemen. You are expected."

They were ushered down a small corridor into a large, wood-panelled waiting room containing leather chairs. "Take a seat please gentlemen. Mister Sanderson will be with you directly. He is on the phone to the Home office."

Butler took a seat by the window, he was sure that they would be being observed and probably recorded. He had read somewhere that where you sit in situations like this affect the balance of power in any subsequent discussions. Sanderson was a powerful man but he needed to know that Butler meant business.

Davis was peering intently at the painting that hung over the marble fireplace. "Any idea what it is supposed to be of?" he asked. The bookcase swung open, taking him by surprise.

"It is a Chagall" A girl in a long turquoise dress moved effortlessly into the room "Reichenbach is a big supporter of the arts. Would you gentlemen like a drink while you are waiting?"

Davies perked up at the offer. "A cup of tea wouldn't go amiss darling." Her mouth smiled while her eyes hardened.

"What kind of tea would you like, sir? we have most of them." Butler noticed the emphasis on the sir.

Davies seemed oblivious to the slight but baffled by the question. "Tea," he said "Rosy lea. Builders tea. Milk and three sugars. Tea"

She smiled indulgently as if she were dealing with a small child. "And for you sir?"

"Earl Grey?"

"Of Course"

"What is a Chagall?" said Davies after she had left the room. "An awfully expensive painting," said Butler "Designed to show us that we are in the halls of the mighty."

A tall bespectacled man appeared in the doorway. "Actually," he said softly "Fine Art is something we invest in on behalf of our clients. This particular one makes a nice centrepiece for the room although it is not to my taste."

"No," said Butler " a little too sentimental for me" Davies looked at him as though he had just begun speaking Martian. "DI Butler by the way. This is Sergeant Davies."

Sanderson shook each of them by the hand and directed them into his office where their drinks were set out in bone china mugs. The girl in the turquoise dress was hovering, pouring the tea.

"Thank you, Jasmine," he said, "We can take it from here." They watched as she left the room. "My assistant" he explained "Can be a little over the top. Now, how can I help you, gentlemen? I believe that you are from the Sussex constabulary.

I have a home in the county so I am eager to assist you with anything you might need."

"We are working on a series of fraud cases in conjunction with the National Crime Agency." Butler began "One of which involves the sale of Spanish apartments off-plan operating from a shopfront in Brighton.

Upon investigation, we find that the shop is owned by your fund and that your fund is also a significant shareholder in the operation."

Sanderson raised an eyebrow "OK. Let me just check with the oracle." If he was disturbed at all by the information it did not show. He tapped at a keyboard concealed in his desk.

"One way and another we own quite a lot of retail property in Brighton," he said. "Ah. There we are. Makepeace Terrace?" Butler nodded "and the tenant name?"

"Estados Development"

"Ah yes," Sanderson seemed pleased with his ability to negotiate the system. "Mr Fisher. I met him the other day but I didn't make the connection."

"Since Michael Fisher is our principal suspect in this investigation, I hope you won't mind my asking the circumstances in which you met him."

"Absolutely not. It was at a drinks party at my house. May I put that in context? It might be useful to your investigation if you have the answer to the question - what does Reichenbach actually do?. The glib version is that we manage our clients' investments but it covers a far wider spectrum of activity.

In some cases, we are simply fund managers, managing investment portfolios for, for example, pension funds. In other cases, our clients invest a certain amount of money which we then manage to seek above-market returns.

We have a range of funds that offer different risk profiles ranging from core funds that invest only in blue-chip companies for example through to opportunity funds where returns are expected to be higher to compensate for higher risk exposure.

In total, we have around four hundred billion sterling of funds under management globally. You might find it hard to imagine but that only makes us a medium-sized player in this market. Makepeace Terrace is a real estate investment that sits in one of our added-value funds and our stake in Estados is held in one of our opportunity funds."

"So they are reckoned to be risky?"

"All risk is relative. If a project had a very risk of failure we wouldn't touch it. Estados is mid-ranking. It has a good chance of creating real value. That brings us back to your original question about Michael Fisher.

Every few months we hold a reception of some kind both for existing clients and those that we would wish to become clients.

It has become customary to invite representatives from some of our projects to emphasise how important the backing of Reichenbach is.

On the occasion in question, it was at my house in Sussex and Michael Fisher was invited along to talk to potential investors."

Butler nodded "Can you tell us what was discussed?"

"Well, as I am sure you know Detective Inspector, these things are a bit of a whirl. There are hundreds of people: politicians, ministers, your own Assistant Chief Constable attended - a lovely man. My objective is to greet everyone and meet them again in the course of the event. As I recall, we talked briefly about the progress of the project but these events are not the forum for that. I believe we also talked about Brighton and Hove Albion's progress in the Premier League. Might I ask a question?"

"Please"

"What is it that Michael Fisher is suspected of doing? And, as a supplemental, how you think that we at Reichenbach might be involved in whatever it is?"

Davies had been sitting silently throughout the meeting but this, he felt, was his moment. "Deposit-taking," he said.

"Given that the project involves selling villas off-plan, isn't that just par for the course?"

"That depends," said Davies "the word on the street is that it is a scam and the deposits will just disappear."

That raised eyebrow again. "Let me just pull up the risk assessment." Sanderson tinkered with the keyboard. "We undertake a key man assessment for all our projects."

Davies wasn't finished. "Why did you choose that particular company to invest in? It is a bit below your usual game isn't it?"

Sanderson smiled. "That question requires a detailed explanation. Let's deal with Michael Fisher first. As part of the assessment we investigated his financial history, his digital history and, of course, we had a CRB check done. It looks to me as though he is as clean as a whistle apart from some minor offences committed when he was a juvenile. There would have been no warning bells at all from this report. As to why we invested. Your assumption that Estados would be too small for us is generally correct, save for the fact that, in the interests of balancing risk, we deliberately pick a few projects every year with a different profile and hold them in an SPV.

This is one of those. All our investments are evaluated thoroughly and passed to our investment committee who sign it off, or not as they see fit."

"SPV?" Davies was confused

"Special Purpose Vehicle – in this case, a company called Trizer"

"Isn't that unusual? Why not hold it directly?"

"Not at all. It probably applies to around a third of our real estate investments. It is purely an administrative convenience."

"But where did the opportunity to invest come from?" Butler tried to pick apart the answer " Who brought it to you?"

More tinkering with the keyboard. "We keep our ear to the ground all the time. Of course. It came from a Spanish broker called Juvenal. We get this sort of approach all the time, it comes with the territory of being one of the bigger players. We pay them a finder's fee as a percentage of the end value of the investment."

"And, if you don't mind me asking, what might that end value be?"

Sanderson checked again "We estimated it would be three hundred million, but the market has fluctuated a little in the intervening period."

"Three hundred million pounds?"

"Euros. It could be more than that. A lot depends on the quality of the golf course."

"Does the name Mijas mean anything to you?"

Sanderson smiled "Juan Mijas? Of course. What has he been up to now? I had dinner with him a week or so ago."

Butler could feel the power in the meeting slipping away. "Could you explain the nature of your relationship with Senor Mijas?"

"Have you heard of an organisation called Far from Home? It is a charity that supports refugees. I have the privilege of being an ambassador for them. Mainly this is to do with raising funds. As you probably know, Juan Mijas, in addition to being a prominent regional politician in Spain, is also heavily involved in the local football club. At my suggestion, he is arranging a charity match against a team made up entirely of refugees or their families. As you can imagine that includes some big names. I am selling tickets if you are interested? they are quite pricey but it all goes to a good cause."

Butler shook his head "Above my pay grade I am afraid. So you went to Spain to set up a football match."

Juan invited me over to meet his team. We visited the ground and had dinner at a charming little restaurant in the hills. I flew back the next morning."

"You mentioned a finder's fee. What sort of percentage would that be?"

"I believe in this case it is fifteen per cent. That is a lot higher than we usually go, but Juvenal is a long-standing contact and has come good in the past."

* * *

As the taxi made its way back to Victoria, Davies seemed stunned by the interview.

"I have spent my career as a copper locking up villains for nicking stuff worth peanuts. The biggest job I can remember is a load of scrap metal worth a couple of hundred grand. Unless we stop them, these bastards are going to get away with thirty million."

Butler looked up from his notes "A sight more than that I think. They will pay nothing for the land, they will have the cash paid upfront by our good citizens and people will be falling over themselves to buy villas there. Thirty is just incidental expenses."

"We are in the wrong job" Davies sighed. "I think the time is right to start rolling up some of these villains. I know they are only small beer but it's an affront to my dignity to leave them carrying on ripping people off."

Butler nodded "OK. Mickey Fisher first – then the hangers-on. Arrange for the heavy squad to go shopping."

Raoul

Rio was getting bored with Malaga. It was a working city and an important port but tourists still dominated every aspect of living there. She sensed a certain desperation in the relentless attempts to create a party atmosphere. Something that seemed so easy in places like Mykonos or Ibiza here seemed hard work.

Then there was Anya. Although the sex was good, intellectually Rio found her challenging. Little things had begun to irritate her about Anya. Perhaps it was to do with her command of Spanish - at best basic and limited to the kind of vocabulary that one might find in a restaurant. But then there was a body to die for...and those eyes.

She missed Madrid. She missed her favourite restaurants and coffee shops. She missed being able to pop into the Prado at lunchtime. She missed the sheer heft of the place.

After a quick kiss, Anya had left for the restaurant. She worked four nights on then three off, so Rio would see little of her until the weekend.

from Baltasar's description, she wasn't looking forward to meeting Raoul. It shouldn't be a problem, she reasoned, anyone who had spent a couple of years in the drug squad knew his type and would be well used to dealing with his kind - as sternly as necessary.

The blond wig was itching. "Guys like this like a bit of skirt." Baltasar was old school. He had spoken to Raoul on the phone and felt able to offer sartorial advice. "He thinks you are a reporter – dress like one."

Rio didn't wear skirts. Her compromise was her best trouser suit and this bloody wig that she had borrowed from Anya.

The last time she had worn a wig was to a party three years before. It didn't help her to pick up anyone then and she doubted that it would help now.

The traffic had been appalling and the drive from Anya's apartment had been fractious, even to a seasoned Madrileno like Rio, with much screeching of brakes and sounding of horns. The americano was very welcome as she relaxed into her seat and waited for Raoul to appear.

At the appointed hour there was no sign of him. She understood that it was all a power play - making her wait on his pleasure. He was probably watching. She yawned and ordered another coffee.

He was even worse than even she expected. Tall and swarthy, he worked out a bit and loved showing off his musculature in a sleeveless shirt slightly too small for him. He walked with his hips forward as though showing off his crutch.

Rio smiled sweetly "Good afternoon – Raoul I presume?" He grunted a reply. "You are selling some photographs I believe?"

Raoul rocked back on his heels, unable to believe his luck. "I wasn't expecting them to send a chick" he breathed, switching into seduction mode. "I mean this is pretty heavy. Guys kissing guys and other stuff." He sat down heavily next to her spilling the half-drunk americano.

Rio couldn't resist a little goading. "Does it turn you on?" Raoul put his head back and emitted a long braying laugh. Too long thought Rio. "Can I see the photos? I would like to look at them before I pay."

Raoul glanced around him and moved closer conspiratorially. Rio could smell cheap Moroccan tobacco tempered with sweat. "Not here" he muttered "You have the five thousand?"

Rio knew full well that Baltasar had agreed four thousand over the phone. She shrugged

"I can get it – once I have seen the pictures"

Raoul behaved as if she had insulted his mother "You don't have the money?" He half-screeched and half-whispered. "You don't have the money? We had a deal."

"Yes - at four thousand. If you want the money show me the pictures."

Raoul turned away melodramatically. "Four thousand? Well bitch, the price just went up"

"Perhaps they are worth five thousand – show me."

Raoul stood and drew himself up to his full height. "or maybe more. Come with me."

As she got up Rio eased the strap off her holster. Better safe than sorry. Raoul led the way out of the café and around the side of the building.

Once in the courtyard at the back of the building he reached into his inside pocket and pulled a couple of photos out of an envelope.

"Just a sample. You see the rest when I have the six thousand."

In her years in the *Brigada social*, Rio had seen far, far worse. The grainy pictures were, she guessed, taken with a mobile phone, probably for the specific purpose of blackmail.

Two naked men kissing. A much younger man kissing an older guy. Two guys humping. What was interesting however was the identity of the older man – Julio Parador, Mijas' Head of Planning.

Raoul's expression had turned into a greedy leer. "Hot stuff eh?"

Rio shrugged and smiled. "I have seen worse." From her perspective, the next step was to either pay him the four thousand euros in her handbag then take the rest of the photos – with or without his agreement.

Alternatively, she could show him her badge and draw her weapon before arresting him.

"You like seeing guys naked?"

"I prefer girls." She knew that it was the wrong thing to say if there was to be no violence - but she had had enough of Raoul.

Raoul raised an eyebrow. She guessed that it would be an affront to his masculinity and she was right.

"I never met a lesbian that didn't long for sex with a man," he said. Rio laughed cynically.

Raoul, on the other hand, saw the laugh as some kind of acquiescence. "How about you suck my dick as a down payment" he suggested, grabbing the journalist's blond hair - trying to force her to her knees.

Later, reflecting on the afternoon's events from the relative safety of the hospital bed he was handcuffed to, Raoul was struggling to think of the point at which he realized that he was out of his depth.

Thinking back, he should have realized that the reporter policewoman lesbian had remained icy calm throughout their encounter, despite his clumsy attempts to intimidate her.

He blamed his nose. When he was a teenager he had once crashed a stolen moped and, in the process, smashed it on a kerbstone. Ever since then, if anyone touched it, it bled profusely and worse his eyes instantly produced floods of tears rendering him unable to see. If it hadn't been for his nose he would have nailed her. She had been lucky.

His first surprise was the beautiful mane of golden hair that he found in his right hand. The second was the palm heel strike that opened up his nose like an over-ripe tomato. He flailed around blindly clutching the wig to his nose to stem the blood until a snap kick to his groin brought the unequal contest to a close.

His last blurry view before the pain from his testicles overwhelmed him was of a harridan with cropped dark hair crouching in front of him like a cat as he fell at her feet.

Rio slipped the clip back on her holster before pulling Raoul's arms behind him and cuffing them together. She reached into his jacket pocket and took out the envelope, wiping off the blood dripping from his face.

As she stood Raoul aimed a kick which she blocked with an elbow strike causing him to howl in pain. She smiled ruefully.

"I would stay still if I were you"

This sort of combat was normally enjoyable – assuming she had a worthy opponent. Nevertheless, it made the tedium of Malaga worthwhile. Since leaving the GOE she was usually restricted to fighting in the gym rather than on the streets.

Raoul groaned and scrabbled around, trying to get up. "Crazy bitch. What are you doing?"

Rio produced her badge and held it in front of his face.

"I am detaining you for questioning.

As you seem to be injured I will arrange for you to be taken to hospital initially."

"I don't need any hospital." Raoul rolled onto his side.

"You don't understand. I am not sending you to hospital for your benefit, although the thought of the doctors displaying your damaged undercarriage to their students is quite appealing.

I am sending you so that your injuries can be recorded by an independent third party. That way, when you accuse me of attacking you, as your lawyer will surely recommend, it will accord with my account of fending off your sexual assault."

Raoul swore vocally. "This is racism. You attacked me because I am Moroccan."

Rio rolled him over onto his back with her boot. "Where did you get the photographs?"

Raoul was started to gather his senses. His nose had almost stopped bleeding and the pain in his groin had resolved itself into a dull ache.

"What photographs? The ones you planted on me?"

Rio placed her boot on his crutch and transferred her weight briefly. Raoul screamed in pain. "Jacob. I got them from Jacob."

"See, that was easy, wasn't it? Jacob who?"

"I don't know."

Rio transferred her weight again to further screaming.

"Please. I don't know. He lives on the beach. Please leave me alone."

"Stay down" Rio stepped back and took the photos out of the envelope and began to inspect them. Raoul adopted the foetal position and waited for the nightmare to end.

After a while, Rio put them back in the envelope. "OK. They might be useful," she said.

"I bet they are making you horny, bitch" hissed Raoul. "where is my five thousand?"

This time Rio laughed out loud. "You don't even have the brains to know when you have been beaten do you?" she said, "Unless you want to try again?"

Raoul's body began to heave with sobs "please don't hit me again"

"I bet you took the pictures yourself. They are of such poor quality that I don't think any payment would be appropriate."

Rio took out her mobile phone. The first call was to the local police. It was always better to let them record any arrest out of courtesy if nothing else.

"Good afternoon. This is Inspector Dos Rios of the Cuerpo Nacional. I am at the junction of Faro and Reding.

I need some assistance with the apprehension of a suspect. He is not armed and I don't think he is dangerous.

It is nothing much but he was resisting arrest so he will need a doctor to look at his injuries."

Baltasar was waiting for her next call.

"What do we have?"

Rio was looking through the photographs again, "Gay sex mostly but a clearly identifiable Parador with what looks like a minor."

"Looks like it is time we paid him a visit."

The third call was to Anya to see what time she might be back. After all, she reasoned, while she was in Malaga there had to be some compensations and, oddly, Raoul had been quite right.

Closure

Mickey was sipping a margarita on a sun lounger whilst several beauties splashed around in the swimming pool. Derek Sanderson was introducing them to him one by one. They were all naked. An irritating ringing sound was interrupting things.

He reached over and grabbed his mobile from the bedside cabinet.

"Did I wake you?"

He raised his head off the pillow to see the alarm clock. It was five-thirty. The bed was empty. Sharon had decamped to the spare room for some reason.

"Not really" He recognised the languid tones of Jasmine.

"I was lying here thinking of you and how nice it would be to meet up again."

He smiled. This had to be a wind-up.

"That would be nice. Where are you?"

"I am kicking my heels in Torremolinos. Derek sent me away."

"He doesn't know what he is missing"

"His wife needed him at home for a few days. He thought it would be good for me to go on holiday, though why he picked this dump I don't know."

"Sounds like a waste to me"

"Anyway, I am at a loose end. There is nothing to do here. I have no one to talk to and shagging Spanish waiters is not my thing. I wondered if you could stay on for a few days."

Mickey was starting to get confused. "I am in Brighton."

Jasmine laughed "Sorry. I was supposed to give you a message. Derek says shut down the UK operation ASAP and move it to Torremolinos as discussed. I presume you know what he is talking about?"

"Yes"

"Then I will make arrangements for a flight, car and so on and text you the details. I already have a hotel room big enough for us both."

"I can't wait"

"Who was that?" Sharon was standing bleary-eyed in the doorway of the bedroom "I had to get away from your snoring" she said by way of explanation.

"Just work," he said, getting out of bed "I need to get in early this morning."

* * *

He was waiting in the office when Dominic arrived.

"Something wrong?" he asked as he came in, surprised to see him.

"No Dominic. Nothing is wrong. It all went extremely well but all things come to an end."

Dominic noticed the past tense. "Does that mean I am being sacked?"

"Yes, I am going to terminate your employment, but I am also going to give you a bonus as well as paying up your contract. We are going to close down this office completely today. Are you OK to help me with that?"

Dominic shrugged "Obviously I don't have anything else to do."

"Right. The first thing we need to do is shut the blinds and put a notice on the door. What we don't want are any existing customers getting agitated that their deposits have disappeared."

"Are they going to disappear?"

"No of course not. Everything is protected as you have been telling them over the last few days. Estados is still running - it's just that it makes a lot more sense to run it from Spain as we move into the development phase full-time. I need your help with the office equipment. I have a company coming to take it away but they can't do this morning for some reason. I am going to take the hard disk out of the server to Spain with me. I need to leave them a contact. Someone who has a key."

"What sort of bonus did you have in mind?"

"How does two hundred sound?"

"Not enough. I am not completely stupid. I understand that the customers trust you to look after their deposits. I just don't understand why - especially when you are closing down their main point of contact without notice."

"Four hundred?"

"Call it a grand, in cash, and I will stay here until they come for the machines."

Mickey could see that his plan to leave Dominic to carry the can had started to leak badly. Reaching inside his jacket he opened his wallet and counted out one thousand pounds in fifties.

"I thought you were a clean pair of hands" he muttered

"I am - but this is every man for himself"

* * *

He drove slowly past the lock up a couple of times before parking the Jag in front of number seven. Nobody knew about it and he wanted to keep it that way. There were no signs that he could see that anyone had been interested in any of the units. He had installed a video camera that covered the apron in front of the garages linked to a website and he had monitored the video feed for the last few days. Apart from the guy who rented the adjacent garage, no-one had been near nor bye.

He reversed the Jag into the space and shut the garage doors. Sitting in the comfort of the padded leather seat he ticked off the things he had to do in his mind. The office was now closed and Dominic was in place. There was no company coming to pick up the computers – his instructions were just to take the disk and write off the rest. Despite a cavalier approach to life generally, Mickey never underestimated the police and in the last few days, he had almost felt their hot breath on his collar. He guessed that arresting Dominic would give him a few extra hours at least.

They might well arrest Sharon as well. She was the last item on his to-do list. He couldn't summon up the courage to tell her to her face that it was over. He was off to Spain and he couldn't see himself returning any time soon. Thinking back the only things that Sharon knew for sure would be things that would incriminate her as well as him, so he judged it unlikely that she would tell the police very much – unless they gave her some kind of deal of course, in which case she would probably sing like a bird.

Much as he liked Sharon he was aware that she had a vindictive streak. It was likely that she would take the split badly and would be seeking revenge. That might become uncomfortable.

The garage was quite spacious, but having the Jag inside made it a bit cramped and he struggled to get around the whole car as he covered it with the tarpaulin.

He opened the floor safe and pulled out his second passport. Whether it was to flee the wrath of irate fathers or the long arm of the law he didn't know but years ago he had planned how to disappear.

Having an Irish grandfather he found that he was entitled to a passport. His father had anglicised the surname to Fisher but Michael had opted for the original Gaelic and was now documented as Michael Ó Bradáin.

He had a feeling that it might be useful in the coming years. Also in the safe were his emergency funds, credit and debit cards - enough to spirit him away when the time came and that time was getting closer.

He stepped out of the garage and locked the door before walking quickly in the direction of the station. He had just over two hours before his flight and Gatwick was at most forty-five minutes away.

"Fisher isn't it? Mister Fisher?"

He groaned inwardly but turned back smiling. It was one of the couples that he had persuaded to sign up "Mr and Mrs Turner isn't it? How are you?"

"We are just champion. Waiting for our new villa to be ready so we can move in."

"You are in Phase One I believe? It will only be a matter of weeks now. I don't have the detailed completion schedule with me but if you pop into the office Dominic will show it to you. "

205

"We'll do that. Thanks. Where are you off to? Not running off with our money are you?"

Mickey laughed "You got me! South America here I come! I am actually on my way to Spain right now to check on progress and my flight leaves fairly soon so I need to catch a train."

"Oh well. We won't keep you"

"Lovely to see you both looking so well. Don't forget to look into the office if you have any questions. Come to think of it Dominic was leaving early today. So probably best leave it until tomorrow."

* * *

Dominic was bored. He had been waiting for at least two hours for the equipment to be collected and he had had enough. If, as he thought, Mickey had run off with the money, he wouldn't be back to check on him and he could leave with impunity despite taking the thousand pounds.

If he was going to walk out, it would be a shame to leave without at least a laptop. Since they were all going to be collected anyway, he was sure that one wouldn't be missed. He browsed around the office seeing what else might be available.

In one of the desk drawers, he found a new iPhone still in its box. He took it out and put it in his pocket along with the charger and earbuds.

He was just putting a computer in his bag when a knock at the door became insistent. He mouthed "Closed" at the two men outside. One of them pressed something against the shop window – it was a warrant card.

"Sergeant Davies, Detective Constable Walters. You are?"

"Dominic. Dominic Sharp."

"Are you employed here, Dominic?"

He thought about denying it, after all, he had been sacked.

"Yes and No." He explained that he had been dismissed because the office had closed down permanently and that he was waiting here for someone to pick up the computers and furniture.

Much to his surprise, he found himself sitting in the back of a squad car on the way to the police station. The laptop was in his bag by his feet and he could feel the iPhone in his jacket pocket. His grandmother had always warned him about stealing but she hadn't mentioned justice as instant as this.

* * *

Sharon parked across the road and watched. Number seven was one of a row of identical garages that had long become detached from the shop leases of which they were once a part.

She watched as a white van parked outside number nine and a couple of lads loaded some anonymous brown cardboard boxes inside, all the while looking furtively around them for observers. They could contain anything she thought to herself as could any of the garages. It was an ideal place to store parts of your life that you wanted to remain out of sight.

She remembered a film about the robbery of a bank vault in the West End and how it had resulted in all these shady corners being exposed. There should be a sequel based on the opening up of a row of garages.

The door to number seven was slightly ajar and she could see lights inside. If this were a film she would go and peer in the open door and get spotted by the baddies but instead she sat and watched.

Once the van had gone all was quiet. She was about to get out of the car when the garage door swung open and Mickey stepped out. He was carrying a small overnight bag. She could see the back of his beloved Jag and noted that he had covered it up with a tarpaulin.

She hunched down behind the steering wheel so as not to be seen but Mickey just walked away up the road towards the station. He looked for all the world as if he were going on a business trip.

She thought about following him but she didn't want to leave the car. She let him get to the end of the road then drove slowly in the same direction. She could see him in the distance talking to a couple of people that she half recognised.

She turned off and drove back to the house. Whatever Mickey was doing, clearly she wasn't part of it. Time to set a course that didn't involve him she thought.

Parador

The room was bare apart from a metal table and four chairs. Most of one wall was devoted to a mirror. On the table was a black digital recorder that showed a red light – the only colour in the completely white landscape.

On one of the chairs sat Julio Parador - looking terrified. Baltasar watched through the mirror as he twitched and fidgeted alone in the interview room. He hadn't had much sleep - the drive from Madrid had necessitated an early start – and he was feeling fractious. The door opened silently and Rojo joined him. He was carrying a couple of folders in which all the incriminating photographs had been laid out and notated.

"How is he doing?"

Baltasar turned "I am letting him stew for a while. He seems to be a bit agitated."

Rojo opened one of the files. "It seems that Jacob, the source of the photographs, is available for hire in the gay community. The local police know him well. Each time they pick him up and hand him over to social services, he escapes from wherever they put him and goes back to the beach."

Baltasar gave a low whistle. "How old?"

"Young. Probably too young. He turned up this morning with his brother, made a complaint about being molested by an older man then fled. They think he has probably gone back to Morocco."

"Protecting himself. No wonder Parador was running away. We found a ticket to Havana in his jacket. He was booked on a flight this evening."

Rojo smiled. "Maybe he just fancied a holiday."

"Rio says that the tickets were only booked yesterday afternoon at ten minutes past four. That would be ten minutes after I arranged for this interview."

Rojo nodded knowingly. "By the way, tell Rio that the local police released her friend Raoul without charge. I got the impression that they thought that she had been a little rough with him."

It was Baltasar's turn to smile "Apparently he tried to grab her."

Rojo shook his head "A very bad move."

"She sorted him out and saved the department four thousand euros in the process. You know we are unlikely to be able to prosecute based on these pictures alone. We need Jacob and if he has disappeared to Morocco there is damn all chance of him returning."

Rojo nodded. "I understand, but they may have their uses nevertheless." He opened the door. "I think our Mr Parador is tender enough by now. Shall we?"

* * *

Parador had had a sick feeling in the pit of his stomach ever since he was arrested. Things had been going well for the past few years. Too well it seemed. Apartments had been built, jobs had been created and the provincial economy had grown fast. None of this could have happened without his drive and determination to grant building licences.

If corners had been cut it was hardly his fault and he saw nothing wrong with accepting gifts from grateful builders – after all, everyone was doing it. All along Judge Diamante had been there to keep the do-gooders off his back.

Now he had disappeared and this swarm of *Madrilenos* had descended on them. What did they know about keeping a province working and prosperous? He would take Mijas' advice and bluff it out. Point out some home truths to these interlopers. After all, they had nothing on him. Anyway, nothing that could not be sorted out quietly amongst friends.

But then, Madrid was known for taking a hard line against purely local customs that were not wholly in accord with their rules. He wondered if he should have taken up their offer of legal representation – but that would make him look guilty.

His mind went blank as the door opened. The youngish one in a suit shook his hand.

"Judge Jesus Rojo. Pleased to meet you"

He had heard stories about this crusading Judge from Madrid who was not scared to dispense with centuries of tradition and custom and enforce his view of the law. He shivered involuntarily.

"Are you cold?" The Judge was carrying a folder of papers. "These interview rooms can be a bit chilly but sometimes I prefer it on a hot day." Parador focused on the folder wishing he could see what was inside it. "Thank you for coming in to see me today. I hope it hasn't inconvenienced you at all"

Parador cursed the airlines inwardly. Not one of them had been able to get him on a flight before this evening otherwise he would probably have been well on the way to sunning himself in Cuba right now and out of their grasp.

"Not at all" he responded warmly. "How can I help?"

Rojo and the older one called Baltasar sat down at the table opposite him. Baltasar turned on the recorder and introduced the interview.

"Could you confirm your name and position of employment for the recording?"

Parador complied. Already this was getting much more rigid than he felt comfortable with. Still, that was Madrid all over - formality and procedure over pragmatism and common sense.

"Mr Parador. I am investigating a complaint concerning the granting of building licenses in contravention of the Land Act 2007 and articles 436 to 442 of the criminal code.

To summarise the complaint, it is alleged that building licenses were sold to companies by public officials for development outside the general zoning plan for your province. Do you have any comment to make?"

Parador shrugged. "I am not surprised. I have been a town planner for most of the last thirty years. This kind of complaint is not uncommon and always surfaces at a particular stage of the economic cycle.

When demand for housing is low there is a surfeit of land and developers keep their heads down. When demand is high, land is in short supply and they all compete. If one developer is granted a building licence and another is not it causes bad feeling and complaints are made. It is rarely the case that the developer has paid off officials."

"Rarely? but it does happen?" Baltasar understood the qualification. Some people found it hard to lie consistently.

Parador opened his arms expansively, warming to his defence. "Of course it happens but there are sufficient checks and balances built into the system to identify it readily."

"Could you explain these checks and balances to us? We are not experts in local Government." Rojo played out the fishing line expertly.

"The office of Mayor is responsible for all governance issues. I am just a member of his cabinet but we are all bound by a collective responsibility to the city. Applications for building licenses are always discussed in cabinet – particularly where they may require modification of the zoning plan. Let us not forget, provincial, regional and national authorities all have the right to challenge any licence that is granted."

Rojo was making notes "I see. So any complaint like this would need a majority of the cabinet to be involved in the payments or approve of them. How many cabinet members are there?"

"Seven – we find it more efficient to have fewer councillors. Decisions are made that much more quickly the way the mayor likes it. He tends to discourage debate because it wastes time."

The float was bobbing up and down as Parador approached the beautiful iridescent fly on Rojo's baited hook.

"Of course, and, I suppose that you are all experts in your field of responsibility. That too speeds things up."

Parador nodded "Yes it does. I know next to nothing about waste and the environment, for example, so I defer to the cabinet member with those responsibilities."

Baltasar leant back in his chair. The fish was on the hook. Time to reel him in. "Correct me if I am wrong, but your argument against the complaint is that it is essentially vexatious and that any such event would require wholesale corruption amongst cabinet members to be effective."

"Corruption is a very strong word." Parador was beginning to think he had said too much.

"Maybe but the cabinet is has very few members. You all defer to the expertise of the cabinet member in question without debate because the mayor likes it that way. It would take only one cabinet member to be corrupt for it to be possible."

Parador's expression had changed from one of composure to a mask of incomprehension. How had this bloody policeman from Madrid with no understanding of how things work locally managed to turn this onto him?

"You, you are putting words in my mouth" he stammered.

The judge intervened. "We will need to investigate your financial affairs. I can do this with your co-operation or I can issue a court order. This has the unfortunate consequence that it is a public document and therefore open to scrutiny - by the press, for example."

Mijas had warned him at the outset that the moment would come when bank accounts would be scoured for evidence of illegal payments and shareholdings would be placed under detailed scrutiny. He was confident that he had covered his tracks well enough to avoid awkward questions being asked.

"I am happy to co-operate," he said calmly, seething at the injustice of it all. "Let me know what you want and I will arrange it with my bank."

"Thank you" This judge, at least, was civilized. Perhaps he understood how things worked differently in a city of half a million people rather than one of six million. Rojo leaned forward and switched off the recorder. Parador breathed a sigh of relief. They had nothing.

"There is another matter we would like to discuss with you while we have your attention." Rojo reached for the folder. "Some explicit photographs have come to our attention that appear to show you committing offences contrary to sections 182 and 183 of the criminal code. Please have a look through this folder and tell us what you think – off the record for the moment."

Parador leafed slowly through the photographs. As he did so his self-control began to crumble visibly and he began to shake. His complexion turned an unhealthy grey as the deepest and most precious secret he held was exposed to the sunlight.

Rojo's voice was like molten silver. "Let me give you a brief history of these pictures. One of my officers intercepted them while they were being sold to the press. I assume that you were already aware of their existence since, I imagine, they were used to try and blackmail you."

The little bastard. He had paid him ten thousand euros to destroy these pictures - but he sold them on anyway. The judge continued softly.

"Your sexuality is of no consequence to me or this investigation but I note that you are married with children and I doubt that your wife is aware of this particular hobby. Professionally, I don't see why your reputation would be damaged were it not for one thing – the age of the other participant."

"Eighteen" croaked Parador in panic, "He says he is eighteen."

Baltasar took over. "The fact that he is that young still leaves a man of fifty-four with questions to answer but we also have a complaint of molestation from a boy that I have seen a picture of somewhere before. He hasn't named anyone yet but as soon as we set up an identification parade I am pretty confident that you will be in the frame. What do you think?"

Parador's mouth was working like a fish out of water. Seemingly random words were uttering forth. "I can't" he spluttered "my wife", "my children". He began to cry soundlessly.

Rojo made his move. "I think the time for self-pity is long past. I have a different set of photographs related to matters we were discussing before that you might like to see." He opened the second folder and placed it in from of the distraught Parador. The pictures were those taken by Rio from the kitchen at the cantina.

"I don't make deals Mr Parador, but I have been known to be forgetful. I know that you are receiving money corruptly for signing building licences. I know that you are being used by Mayor Mijas. In the right circumstances, I could even be persuaded that you were acting under duress and were seeking to put matters right.

In that happy event, I might forget where I have put these photographs showing you as a pervert. You will have to declare the money and make your peace with the tax man but are looking at the difference between a ten-year sentence and a quiet retirement. Which would you prefer?"

Parador knew that the game was up "What do I have to do?"

Rojo leaned forward and switched the recorder back on.

Arrests

The banging of the knocker snapped Sharon out of her stupor. Since she had given up working, she had been at a loose end. Mickey had disappeared, presumably to Spain without any indication of when he would return. Tellingly, he hadn't suggested that she accompany him. She had convinced herself that he had another woman on the go - she didn't know who - probably the same tart that he took to Bristol.

She opened the door slowly. Two policemen were on her doorstep. They were both casually dressed, but she knew they were police long before the badges were shown. She had been expecting them for days.

"Sergeant Davies. DI Butler" They made their introductions. "We are looking for Michael Fisher."

"Isn't everybody?" she said, "Come inside - you will upset the neighbours."

She told them everything she knew - well, almost everything. She had worked in the shop for four weeks, helping to set it up. She had managed the sales assistants and processed the paperwork. She explained about the presentations and how they would encourage people to sign up for villas there and then to avoid disappointment in the future. She told them how all monies taken were paid into a separate account for deposits only and gave them the details. She confirmed that Mickey ran the operation and, had just shut it down without consulting the staff or her.

Once they had the deposit account details Davies went out to the car leaving Butler with Sharon. "He will check the bank account to see it's status and put a notice on any activity" Butler explained. "Do you know if Mickey was acting alone or whether he was working for someone else?" Sharon shook her head. She would save that information for later.

"Can you access the Estados system from here?" She nodded, she could get at all the administration systems. "It would be useful if we had a list of staff members and a list of those who have already paid over a deposit."

The logon failed. "It looks like the server is offline," she said.

"How many customers are we talking about?" Butler was getting impatient

Sharon wasn't sure "We have been running the presentations for about three weeks twice a day including weekends. Each session has netted four or five customers at thirty thousand or so per villa"

"So that must be close to eighty multiplied by thirty"

"Nearly two and a half million quid."

Davies emerged from the car shaking his head. "I can't get any sense out of the bank manager because of data protection. He wants us to make an appointment.

The Kenton's have been in touch again. They received a cheque in the post yesterday. They paid for special clearance but it bounced for lack of funds. I think we'll find that the money has gone."

Butler stood to leave. "Since, on your admission, you have been closely involved in what we believe to be a significant fraud I am afraid that we will have to interview you formally at the station. That interview will be under caution so if you have a lawyer you might like to bring him along - shall we say tomorrow afternoon? If Mickey gets in touch in the meantime ring me on this number." He gave her his card.

She was surprised that they hadn't arrested her immediately but watched from the window as they drove off. She noted the anonymous blue Golf parked opposite. They could stay there all night. She wasn't going anywhere.

* * *

"Hardly as white as the driven snow I would suggest" Davies was at the wheel "I don't buy the innocent maiden betrayed story for a minute"

"It is hard to see how she had no inkling of what was going on I admit," said Butler, fiddling with his phone "especially as she is sleeping with him. I would be surprised if he didn't let something slip."

"Still, we will find out. We have her phones tapped and she is being watched. If she knows where Mickey is hiding she is bound to try and contact him"

"Unless she is right and he has left her to carry the can. Either way, I am sure that Sharon Fellows has more to tell us."

"I arranged to visit the bank tomorrow morning by the way. The manager has his head of security coming down for the day. He used to be on the force so when we tell him it is a fraud he should make sure we get all the info we need."

Butler made a face. "In my experience, it won't help us much. We will just spend loads of Her Majesties resources chasing ever-smaller amounts around an infinite loop of accounts until the money disappears altogether."

"If Mickey has gone to Spain, perhaps your big mate can help us"

"Toro? Yes, the thought had occurred to me. I will get in touch with Judge Rojo but first, we need to confirm that he has indeed gone to Spain. Get someone onto the main airports and see if he appears on any of the passenger lists. Start with Malaga. Estados has an office in Torremolinos and it is just down the road."

* * *

Sharon was studying the invitation and browsing information about Reichenbach when the email from Mickey arrived. At first, her heart leapt when she saw who it was from but as she read it she became progressively angrier. It was a long time since she had been dumped and the first time by email. It didn't hurt any less.

"Gutless bastard" she shouted. She knew he had someone else in tow. Survival was now her primary task. The key question was how to let the police know without incriminating herself. She pulled out the card and dialled Butler's number.

"Mickey has dumped me" she snorted. "It says in this email that I should remember all the good times and he wishes me well."

"Does it say where he has gone?"

"Spain. Torremolinos. To run the Estados office."

"When was it sent?"

"Today at seventeen thirty-two."

"That is a bit brutal. How long were you together?"

"Long enough to be worth more than that. I hope you arrest him because if I find him first I won't be responsible for my actions."

"Is there anything else that you can tell us?"

"I was looking through his things and I came across an invitation to an event run last Wednesday week by a company called Reichenbach."

"It is personalized – in Mickey's name?"

"Yes. I remember him going. He told me he was meeting the money. It didn't mean anything to me at the time but I thought that it might be important."

"Thank you. That is very helpful. Have you arranged for anyone to accompany you to the station tomorrow afternoon?"

Sharon had forgotten about the formal interview. "Do we have to wait? I would rather get everything off my chest as soon as possible."

"Entirely your choice. I'll instruct my officers to bring you in and arrange for the duty solicitor. As you may be arrested and cautioned it is probably best."

* * *

Davies and Butler watched the pale-faced young man sitting in the interview room.

"Tell me who he is again" Butler was still thinking about Sharon Fellows. "He doesn't look old enough to be out on his own."

"His name is Dominic Sharp. We found him when we raided the shop. He claims he was waiting for someone to pick up the office equipment and that he knows nothing about the business. Oh, and he had a grand on him in fifties."

Butler whistled "What is he? A drug dealer?"

Davies opened the door "Let's find out."

They turned into the interview room on the other side of the mirror. Dominic smiled weakly as they sat down.

"Detective Inspector Butler and Detective Sergeant Davies. Could you identify yourself for the recording please?"

Dominic repeated his name clearly and precisely. Davies led the questioning.

"Is it OK to call you Dominic?"

He nodded warily.

"If you could answer yes or no for the tape."

Dominic cocked his head, listening intently "Strictly speaking it isn't a tape" he said, "It is solid-state memory but yes, it is OK to call me Dominic."

Davies was fond of the days when Buckland was in charge and they could get away with physical persuasion. He bit his tongue. "Can you start by telling us about the nature of your employment at Estados?"

It was clear that Dominic liked an audience and he waxed on lyrically about the development and the lovely couples that were buying villas until Davies intervened.

"What can you tell us about the other employees?"

"Well, I haven't been there very long but they were all nice to me. Mostly I just did the job and didn't have time to engage in any chit-chat."

"Did you pick up on any names?"

"There was Sharon. She was lovely. She looked out for me."

"Anyone else?"

"Mickey was the boss. He was the one I told I would wait for the people to collect the office equipment.

He was a funny one. He had a bag with him as if he was going on holiday."

"When was this?"

"This morning. I turned up for work as usual but Mickey was already there and he sacked me. There was nobody else in so I suppose they already knew."

"Where did you get the money?"

"From Mickey. It was a bonus for waiting around for the.."

"...people to collect the equipment. Yes, I got that. It was rather a good bonus wasn't it?"

"I hadn't thought about it."

"Weren't you suspicious?"

"Of what?"

"That all was not well with the company."

"Oh, I see. Yes of course, but it was going to carry on in Spain. It wasn't like it was shutting down completely."

Butler broke in "Can I have a word?" he said to Davies "Outside"

* * *

"We are wasting our time with him. No jury is likely to believe that he was involved in anything except being an annoying little prick. Let him go."

"Technically speaking it isn't a tape" Davies mimicked Dominic's voice. "He deserves to go down for that alone."

"As I say just an annoying little prick"

"So, see if I have got this right. Mickey has done a bunk so we can't arrest him. Sharon Fellows is doing her best to shaft Mickey so we don't want to arrest her and we are not going to arrest this one either.

So far the investigation has produced fuck all in the way of results."

Butler shrugged his shoulders "I wouldn't say that. We have probably flushed out a major criminal even if we haven't arrested him.

We have also stopped the citizens of Sussex donating their life savings to a deposit-taking scam."

"I don't know how things go at the NCA but round here we are judged by the number of arrests we make and we haven't made any. I can't see it going down well upstairs."

Ruby my dear

The black-clad figures hugged the wall out of sight of the CCTV camera mounted on a pole just inside the villa's grounds. The driveway up to the villa was lit softly almost to invite callers into the large, ornate building on top of the hill. Jazz was playing softly – "Ruby my dear," thought Rojo as he watched the scene unfolding.

Through his binoculars, Baltasar could see guests mingling around the pool area. Mijas himself was working the crowd, holding brief conversations with each group of well-wishers before moving on to the next cluster. In subdued lighting of the gardens, guards patrolled the perimeter. Seven, according to intelligence, all armed.

If their timing was wrong or they screwed it up somehow, it was enough to make a fight of it. Fireworks were planned for midnight and the arrest for fifteen minutes later.

Mijas was holding a party for his wife's birthday and the enforcement team had watched as, one after another, the limousines of the local business and political aristocracy had swung into the drive and up that hill before pulling right to park.

Arresting Mijas was always going to be a gamble. Arresting him in front of an audience of his peers was bound to provoke protest among his patrons but Parador's evidence was conclusive. Besides, Rojo mused, it might give some of them food for thought if ever they are tempted to err on the side of criminality.

Typically, Rio was leading the arrest and was one of those currently hiding along the wall. Ever since her days in *Grupo*

Operations Especial, she had relished this part of any operation. Besides, she looked pretty chic in black from head to toe.

They had worked out the plan of attack, poring over plans of the villa and its surroundings - in particular where the twenty-strong team would park without raising any suspicions. The area around Mijas estate was largely scrub but along the road, there was a succession of ancient oaks shielding the boundary. On the other side, the estate tumbled down to the water's edge giving a stunning view over El Limonero, the dam holding back the Guadalmedina river, and the road.

"Given the sensitive nature of this project" Rojo had begun "Everything and everyone involved has to be part of our team based here. We cannot risk involving the locals just in case they are inclined to warn the target."

Getting to such a building without announcing their approach would be difficult. Toro couldn't see the problem. He would drive, in convoy, across the dam, up the entrance road and through the main gates with lights flashing and sirens sounding. Nor could he understand why his suggestion caused so much amusement around the team.

"This is not the OK corral" Baltasar explained, "and we don't want a gunfight given the audience of local worthies, amongst whom, incidentally, is the Commissioner of Police."

"Besides" Rio chipped in "One look at your convoy and Mijas would be in his helicopter and away."

Damn. Toro had forgotten the helicopter. Once the convoy came into view on the dam it would be ten minutes, maybe more, before they reached the villa. More than enough time to affect an escape. "We could use our own helicopter" he ventured.

Baltasar grunted grudgingly and studied the map intently. "the only level ground without tree cover seems to be around his helipad. It doesn't leave much room for a cavalry charge."

"What about the lake?"

"He does have a dock down from the house. From the photographs, it doesn't look as though he has anything more than a rowing boat. There is a concession that hires out pedalos on the other side of the lake. Perhaps we could hire twenty of those?" Baltasar hated boats.

Laughing, Rojo refocussed their thoughts. "There are two main problems – being seen and being heard. The road past the estate is not particularly well used except for access to the villa itself so we don't want too many vehicles and certainly not ones that are easily identifiable as police. The idea of approaching via the lake gives us a noise problem. They would hear us coming."

"Suppose we didn't look like police." Lopez had been silent until now – in awe of his new colleagues. "One of our surveillance vans is dressed up in Telefonica colours."

"That works well in the city but there is little around the estate to justify providing cable. What about power? Does the dam have a hydro plant?"

Toro scratched his head. "I don't think so. It is mostly tourists and fishing. I will ring Endesa and find out"

"Nevertheless. It could work. If we dressed up a couple of vans in Endesa colours we could get away with parking them at one end of the dam close to the access road. How far away is the villa from there across country?"

"Ten minutes at most."

Rio could only be impressed by Rojo's contacts. One phone call and everything had been flown from Getafe airbase into Federico Garcia Lorca in an air force transport plane, vehicles and all, and driven the remaining distance in a little over an hour. The vans had been resprayed to look like they belonged to the local power company.

The guests had begun to arrive around ten. By ten-thirty it was completely dark when Rio led her team into the estate. Their objectives were to neutralise any threat to the operation, disable any means of escape and identify the whereabouts of the target. At twelve-fifteen, amidst the firework display, Baltasar and Rojo would knock on the front door and arrest Mijas.

Thus far, intelligence had been good. Although the motion sensors were set around the perimeter they had been turned off because the local wildlife kept activating the alarms. The bodyguards were patrolling around the villa itself. The GOE team spread out – each with a particular task.

From her position in the shrubbery, Rio could see the little Eurocopter about ten metres away. Just beyond it, someone in a flight suit was sitting on a bench smoking. A helmet sat on the seat beside him. Rio reasoned, it would be easiest to disable the pilot first before attempting the helicopter.

It was a pity that the pilot was the villa side of the helicopter well within the lit area. It would be difficult, if not impossible, to approach him unseen. Even a silenced shot would be difficult because of the helicopter in the way. She pondered her options. "Dock secured," said a voice in her ear "Copy garage," said another. The pilot stood and strolled in Rio's direction

228

unzipping his fly "Copter imminent" she said and moved soundlessly to intercept him as he relieved himself.

The fireworks were good enough to keep the attention of the guests and the bodyguards alike. Intelligence was that the display would last for fifteen minutes. Five of the guards had been taken down with no fuss but Rio had lost two of them.

She flattened herself against the wall of the house and peered around the corner. One was standing behind Mijas himself, watching the fireworks, of the other there was no sign. She moved back from the house "Maintain your positions" she said into her wrist mike. "Once the fireworks stop we move in on my orders". She turned towards the front of the house.

It had cost Huertas a fortune to have his new car towed out of the slurry pond then repaired and valeted. He had gone down to the garage to make sure that no-one had scraped the car in the rush to park all those Mercedes. Inexplicably though, the garage had been locked and there had been no sign of anyone guarding it.

He was on his way back to find out what was going on when he saw her. It was the same bitch that caused him to crash his beloved car. His shoulder holster had been specially designed not to spoil the line of his suit. He reached inside and slipped out his pistol. She had also cost him a new suit – he could never get the smell of slurry out of the Armani.

"Bad move," said Lopez from behind him "Drop the weapon." Huertas turned more out of surprise than intent but it was enough to ensure that Lopez fired the taser. The crescendo of the firework display covered Huertas cries of pain.

Rio jogged up "Well done – but I don't remember tasers being mentioned?" Lopez shrugged. "We carry them all the time."

"They tend to be a bit noisy for this type of work – not the tasers, the targets."

Huertas had stopped whimpering and started to get up until he received a backheel to his shoulder from Rio. Lopez sniffed the air distastefully "What is that smell?"

"Another disadvantage of tasers. He has probably crapped himself. I will leave you to cuff him."

As the fireworks finished Baltasar raised the heavy, cast-iron knocker and banged on the front door. Rojo stood outside the line of fire with Toro. The door opened with a bang and a woman ran out "Armed men" she screamed.

Baltasar strode into the hall followed by Rojo and Toro. On the terrace, they could see Rio cuffing Mijas while Lopez dealt with the remaining bodyguard.

"Ladies and Gentlemen" Rojo raised his voice above the hubbub "This is a police search for persons we suspect of committing offences. My name is Judge Rojo. We need each of you to make a statement. We will try not to detain you any longer than is necessary. Please stay in the building and Inspectors Baltasar and Toro will interview you in turn."

"Do you know who I am?" Mijas was incandescent with rage as Rio marched him up to Rojo.

"Mister Mayor" Rojo was not intimidated "I know exactly who you are. Would you prefer that we charge you in front of your friends or would you rather wait until we get to the station?"

"You are finished Rojo" Mijas spat.

Loss adjustment

Jasmine stood dutifully to one side as Sanderson read the text. She could tell he was angry but he always, always controlled himself. In her view, there was nothing more vulnerable than an angry man making emotional decisions.

"Well," he said "He can't say he wasn't warned. He has been breaking the rules too obviously for too long. It was bound to happen at some stage. It is just unfortunate that it was one of our projects that it happened to. Was he the only one arrested?"

"The details are not clear yet. We know about Mijas and several of his employees but as to the others...."

"First things first. Make sure that Fisher has closed the Brighton operation entirely and cleanly.

Second, prepare an options statement for the project from this point forward. As I see it the only two routes are to continue with phase two and brazen it out or to can the whole project and take any losses on the chin. Give it some thought.

Thirdly, call Judge Diamante on a secure line and use your charms to find out how long it will be before he can get Mijas released. The answer to that may inform the other options."

"Do you want me to inform the investment committee?"

"Not yet - no sense in setting any unnecessary hares running - but tell Kevin to vanish and secure the bank accounts. We don't want Mickey thinking he can help himself. "

* * *

"Judge Rojo sends his compliments" The heavily-accented voice sounded elated. "We have Senors Mijas and Parador in custody."

Butler sat down at his desk. "Well done Toro. Were you involved in the operation?"

"Yes. We all were. We gate-crashed his party. It was very James Bond."

"No casualties I hope"

"No. Only his pride perhaps"

"What happens next?"

"The first thing is to move them back to Madrid out of the grasp of the locals who have been protecting them for a long time."

"Do you have any further information on their funding?"

"Not really. I will send you a transcript of the initial interviews. As you have an interest in the results, Judge Rojo suggested that you might like to be present as observers during the interrogation.

We can provide an interpreter."

"That is kind of him. I know Sergeant Davies will be thrilled."

"It will be in a couple of days. I will let you know the timetable."

"Thank you Toro"

"What will I be thrilled about?" Davies was curious.

"Buy some suntan cream and pack your swimming trunks. We have been invited to observe the interrogation of Mijas and Parador."

Davies smiled "I told you we would be over there for the next meeting."

"How is your Spanish?"

Davies looked crestfallen " I hadn't thought of that."

"I am sure we'll get translated transcripts of what is said. We may even get our own translator. I guess it depends on how generous Judge Rojo is feeling."

"I wish he were signing our expenses. It will be as popular as a turd in a swimming pool as far as upstairs is concerned."

* * *

Jasmine hated being the bearer of bad news and her face gave her away.

"Well?" said Sanderson "Tell me"

"I spoke to the agent for the property in Brighton. He says the police were there and they arrested a young man. My spies in the Brighton station tell me it is a Dominic Sharp. They have also arrested Sharon Fellows as part of the same operation"

"Neither of them know anything but that is annoying, nevertheless. What about the options statement?"

"There is more bad news from Spain. I tried to call Judge Diamante as you suggested. I got through to his home and spoke to his cleaner. It might have been her poor Spanish but I understood her to say that he shot himself a few days ago."

Sanderson leant back in his chair and put his hands behind his head. "Have you tried to confirm that?"

"It is very strange. No-one is saying anything. No confirmation and no denial."

"Then we have to assume that it is true. Poor old Hector."

"Precisely. Given those circumstances, the options statement can only come to one conclusion."

"So, the Spanish police have Senors Mijas and Parador in custody. The office in Torremolinos remains operational but Mr Fisher is on his way to close it down." Sanderson sighed "Which police are we talking about? Locals?"

"No, CNP under the direction of Judge Rojo"

He tutted. "A pity. I doubt that they have uncovered our involvement and we need to keep it that way.

If Judge Rojo is involved they will be going after Mijas on corruption charges. In turn, sadly, that means that the building permissions are likely to prove worthless along with any prospect of end value.

What is the balance sheet looking like?"

She flashed a spreadsheet onto the shared screen. "As you can see, we are showing a decent profit at the moment. The deposits taken comfortably outweigh the expenditure so far.

I checked the deposits and it looks as though someone has already dipped into the account before it was secured."

Sanderson's demeanour turned to stone. "Are you telling me we have been robbed?"

"I'm afraid so"

"What is the damage?"

"There have been quite a few smaller transfers, all below the alert threshold. It looks like a million all told"

"Mickey Fisher?"

"It looks like it"

"My gut tells me it is time we withdrew gracefully. I presume your options statement comes to the same conclusion?"

She nodded. "It does".

Sanderson peered at the screen. "Can you prepare me a termination statement bearing in mind remuneration and insurance costs.

I will also need an information pack for the investment committee. It seems a shame to forgo all that value but the risk profile seems to have moved against us."

"What about Mickey Fisher?"

"I am afraid he is expendable. He has a certain native cunning and I don't want him being turned against us – besides he has our money."

"I told him I was waiting for him in Spain."

"I am afraid poor Mickey is going to have to forego the nights of passion that he is expecting. Message him. Tell him you have rented him an apartment and he needs to pick up the key from the office reception."

"Understood."

"Tell him that you have a new phone - I'll let you have the number in a few minutes. Tell him to ring you from the office when he has the key."

"I'll wait until I have the number."

Thank you, Jasmine. Could you step out for a moment. I need to make a couple of calls."

He watched as she glided soundlessly out of the office. He was impressed at her complete lack of emotion.

He reached inside his desk drawer and pulled out an anonymous mobile phone.

"Imperial Insurance?" he asked quietly "Reichenbach. We need to make another claim."

Execution

Rafik checked the piece of paper in the pocket of his overalls. It was the right address. It appeared to be in darkness but that was not uncommon in the cleaning business. He tended to be there when everyone else had either gone home or were yet to arrive. He checked that he had his mop and bucket.

He unlocked the door and switched on the lights – but nothing happened. The first thing he noticed was a smell of gas.

He knew about power failures. They were a regular occurrence in the run-down apartment block he lived in away from the glitz and glamour of the tourist city.

As he investigated the smell of gas became stronger. In the small kitchen, he found the source of the leak. The gas pipe feeding the small water heater had been smashed off the wall. He looked for a tap to turn off the supply but that too had been smashed.

He ran out of the kitchen into the hallway where the air was still sweeter. He would open the windows once he had caught his breath. He could hear the sirens of the approaching appliances outside.

In the hallway was a small package with what looked like a mobile phone taped to it. Rafik had lost his phone a few weeks ago and couldn't afford another.

He leaned over the package trying to see what was. It looked like a smartphone. As he reached for it - it rang.

* * *

The flight to Malaga had been uneventful and, as promised, a car was waiting for Mickey at the desk. Behind the sun visor was an envelope addressed to him. It contained a single sheet of paper. On it was printed a mobile phone number and a printed message "Rented us an apartment. Key is waiting at the reception desk in the office. Ring me on this number when you get inside. Don't keep me waiting too long. Jasmine".

He pictured her long legs and long black hair and imagined the night to come. He stored the number in his phone before setting off for Torremolinos.

The dual carriageway wound through the hills down to the resort. It was a long time since Mickey had visited the Costa del Sol. He must have been eight or nine. They stayed in Torremolinos close to the beach but he couldn't remember the hotel. His parents always said that they would like to move here but it never happened and now they were long gone.

He hadn't liked the heat he remembered. The temperature in the car showed thirty degrees and it was seven in the evening. He turned the air-conditioning up a notch. By nine o'clock it would all be done and he could look forward to spending his share of the proceeds. Before he left he had made sure that the accounts were fully paid up as he had been promised.

As he drove he considered his options. Sharon would want him to go straight, he did not doubt that, and in some lights not having to keep looking over your shoulder was attractive. The problem was he liked the craic and that was not negotiable- perhaps it was Sharon that was optional. Although he had dumped her he was sure that he would be forgiven.

He pulled into the parking garage and took a ticket. He opted to carry his bag rather than leave it in the car. The heat hit as he stepped out of the garage into the evening sun. Although it was still early, crowds of inebriated tourists were in transit between beach and hotel and he felt overdressed by comparison.

He finally reached Mercedes and began to walk along to the office. Ahead he could see the blue flashing lights of a fire engine. As he got closer he could see the road was taped off and temporary no smoking signs had been placed on the pavement. He could smell gas and could see people being led from the buildings along each side of the street.

Mickey was on high alert. He didn't believe in accidents or coincidences. This was suspicious. The office was on the first floor in the first block inside the cordon. The police had the whole building surrounded.

As it stood, he couldn't reach the office to disable the system, retrieve any cash paid as deposits and remove the hard disk from the server. The only police he could see were uniformed officers trying to marshal the traffic away from the scene. He needed to tell Jasmine that he would be delayed.

* * *

"I thought we agreed that timing was imperative." Baltasar was on the point of losing his temper "Seven o'clock and that is the earliest you can make a move." He put his hand over the receiver and swore. "Seven o'clock it will have to be then. My officers will attend the raid alongside you."

"Problem?" Rojo smiled

"The locals are completely unable to provide officers until seven. Something to do with changing shifts."

"Let us hope that the bad guys are sufficiently uninformed about our arrests yesterday and don't take any action."

"I think it is genetic. Down here they have evolved to move more slowly than everyone else.

Anyway, we have had the place under surveillance all day and Iberdrola ensured that the power failed in that building first thing."

Rojo raised an eyebrow "How did you manage that?"

"Better you don't know officially" Baltasar adopted his confidential tone "My brother is the regional manager. They have a long-term project to replace some kit in Calle Mercedes, he just arranged to bring it forward to today. I gather the notification to the municipal authority got lost in the post."

"That should mean that they have been unable to remove anything and unable to delete anything. Will you be needing some company?"

"If you fancy an evening raiding an office you are welcome to come along. I will be going on my own.

Toro is taking Lopez to escort the transfer of our prisoners to Madrid in the morning and Rio is riding shotgun."

* * *

Mickey turned down an alleyway, selected the number and pressed the dial button.

The explosion was instantaneous, showering the street where he had been standing with broken glass. For an instant he was stunned. The sound of car alarms triggered in the shock wave echoed around the narrow alleyway.

He peered around the corner. Where the windows of the office had been there was a blackened hole. Flames licked upwards from the broken main. Bodies lay in the rubble and the fireman next to whom Mickey had been standing was sitting slumped against a car, thrown there by the blast.

That the explosion had been targeted at him was, in his mind, without doubt. The message had been clear "Ring this number when you get inside the office".

If he had been inside the office he would be dead. No question. His well-honed survival instincts kicked in.

With luck, it would be assumed that he had followed instructions. It would take some time, hours at least, probably days to identify the victims by which time he needed to be well hidden.

He lobbed his phone into the street, walked quickly down the alley, through the foyer of a hotel and out onto Bajondillo. The danger points would be the hire car, the hotel where he was supposed to be staying and the airport. All of these were to be avoided.

He joined the crowds moving up towards the town. Ducking into a clothing shop he first bought himself a loud shirt, a pair of shorts and some fit flops, using the changing room to pack his clothes into the suitcase.

Michael Ó Bradáin the tourist emerged and strolled back into town towards the station. He stopped at a phone shop and bought himself a new phone, paying in cash as the sirens of emergency vehicles created a cacophony of noise washing around the narrow streets.

* * *

"I swear the traffic gets worse on this coast every year"

Baltasar and Rojo had not moved for five minutes. A uniformed traffic officer strolled past and Baltasar flashed his badge to find out what was going on.

"They have cordoned off part of the centre because of a gas leak. If you have a blue light, use it and I will try and create some space for you but it will be difficult."

Rojo checked his phone "It is probably best to park up and walk. We have time"

The policeman directed them onto a private forecourt. "Technically it is illegal but I will make sure you don't get towed"

The two men stood out against the crowds of tourists as they walked towards the centre as swiftly as the temperature allowed.

They were halted by a fireman who refused to allow them any further. "Calle Mercedes is cordoned off for safety reasons," he said and even Baltasar's rank failed to move him. "We need to secure the area before anyone goes in."

Before Baltasar could argue the point the explosion lit up the street a hundred metres away. The fireman stood paralysed with shock as Baltasar began running towards the site.

"Come" shouted Rojo "They need your help" The fireman didn't, couldn't move.

Rojo slapped him. "Come" he repeated and, taking his arm, they stumbled off after Baltasar who was attending to the first body he found.

* * *

The train to Marbella took an hour and a quarter. Mickey took advantage of the time to change back into his clothes and load up his new phone. He was as sure as he could be that he wasn't being followed. He rang ahead to book another car.

It was time for the escape hatch and he had a route planned out in his mind. The problem was that he hadn't planned on starting from here. He had taken everything he needed from the lockup. The question was how to get away from Marbella without being seen.

He thought about Gibraltar – too many eyes and ears; he thought about Seville – too small an airport; and opted for Lisbon. The sat nav told him that it was seven hours away. He booked an early morning flight to Amsterdam. It was going to be a long night.

* * *

"One dead. Seven injured." Baltasar swore "If that was a genuine gas leak…" he tailed off as his phone rang. Rojo didn't normally drink beer but after spending an hour trying to help the wounded he needed it badly and he drank deeply of the ice-cold lager.

Baltasar put his phone down on the table. "That was the fire investigator. They found the remains of a small device. From the preliminary analysis, it looks like it was triggered remotely by a mobile phone. They are fingertipping the remains to see if they can find anything else."

"So If it was deliberate. Why? Just to get rid of evidence? Or maybe to get rid of somebody. Do we know anything about the victims?"

"Mostly tourists from the look of them. The body is unidentifiable so far because of the explosion. It is too badly burned. All they would say is that it is male."

"As far as we know all our suspects and witnesses are accounted for?"

Baltasar shrugged. "The ones that count are in jail."

"We had better make sure they are safe" Rojo took another swig of beer. "Are we missing something here? We didn't expect to find anything very much at the sales office. It seems pretty heavy-handed to blow up the office."

"I fear it was to stop us. You and me. Another few minutes and we would have been with a search team in that office."

"So you think that they thought we were there."

"Did you see hide or hair of the locals when we arrived? Remember we were late on the scene. I would have expected them to have been there already."

"And they would have expected us to be there"

Baltasar finished his beer and stood angrily "I have had enough of this shit. If I find that they have been sharing information with the other side. I will see to it that heads start rolling."

"I should check first. It may be that they have a good reason for not being there. Let me make a polite enquiry before you start shooting."

Baltasar's phone rang again "and you didn't think to pass that information on to us? I am not impressed." He put the phone back on the table and let out a long sigh. "It seems they were notified of the gas leak and aborted the operation. They just didn't think to share it with us."

Proudfoot

As they climbed the stairs, Butler noticed that Davies had adopted the demeanour of a naughty schoolboy approaching the headmaster's study with every expectation of being caned.

"What I said about the shit hitting the fan? This is the exception. The word is that he is pissed by our lack of arrests."

Butler nodded. "So we expect a bollocking."

"It's all right for you. You can just swan off back to The NCA. I have to stay here and take it."

Proudfoot was standing by the window with the phone glued to his ear when they entered his office. He was red in the face and almost spluttering with rage. He barely acknowledged them as he tried to interject with whoever was on the other end of the line.

"I think if I may say so sir that is most unfair but I will consider what you say. Preserve my pension. Yes Sir. Thank you, sir." He placed the phone carefully back on the receiver than sat down heavily at his desk and sat in silence.

After a significant pause, Butler made the first move "You asked to see us, sir?" The noise had a galvanising effect and Proudfoot sat bolt upright glowering at the two officers.

"As the ranking officer in this room I control the conversation" he snarled. "Now. One of you idiots can perhaps enlighten me as to what in the name of holy fuck is going on."

"We are making progress in our investigation," said Butler

"No" Proudfoot drew himself up to his full height. "No. Don't you dare give me any of that sanitised shit. It was perfectly simple. We had a scam operating from a shop in our territory. We knew who was operating it. All you had to do was to arrest him and move on but when I enquire how things are going I find that the shop is shut and our suspect has fucked off to Spain taking the money with him while you two stood by watching. What part of that is progress?"

"With respect, it is a much more complex case than you imagine sir"

"Did you hear that Sergeant?" Davies almost flinched when Proudfoot's attention turned to him. "With respect. People always say that before they are going to be bloody rude. I can imagine that this interloper thinks that he knows better than simple country policemen but I am surprised at you Davies. I thought you knew better."

"Sergeant Davies has behaved professionally throughout this investigation and followed my orders to the letter."

"So what's this? Mea Culpa? I got it wrong sir. With respect."

"No Sir. I think your anger is misplaced."

"Misplaced?"

The door opened quietly and Amanda Smallbone stepped into the room distracting him. "Ah." He said, "Brutus arrives to slip another knife into my ribcage."

"Oh stop being so melodramatic John. The game is up. You know it. They know it. Just let it rest. I take it you have spoken to the Chief Constable?"

Proudfoot nodded "It was made clear to me that I was resigning with immediate effect and that you were stepping up temporarily." His voice wilted "I still don't know why"

Smallbone caught Butler's eye "Do you want to explain"

"The complexity of this, apparently simple, case lies in the funding of the operation. Our enquiries show that the owner both of the shop and the company are a large investment fund called Reichenbach. Reichenbach is run by a man called Derek Sanderson who is, I believe, known to you."

Proudfoot's jaw dropped and he sat down. "Derek is a long-standing friend" he stammered "I can't believe that he would be involved in a cheap deposit-taking scam. I mean the man is a churchwarden and captain of the golf club."

"It was being used as a means to a much bigger prize."

"But he has an enormous house. He is rich. Why would he? And what have I got to do with it?"

"I will take it from here" Smallbone intervened. "Sergeant Davies what we are about to discuss is extremely confidential. I will understand if you want to excuse yourself but if you stay not a word of what we say will leak from this room on pain of your bollocks being hacked off with a rusty pair of scissors."

Davies looked completely stunned by events. "I'll stay Ma'am" he gulped, impressed with her imagery.

"Derek Sanderson is not only a suspect in this investigation but also in parallel cases with Fraud, HMRC and the anti-terrorist team at the Met. DI Butler was seconded to us from the NCA primarily to pursue the links between our little scam and Sanderson's organisation."

Proudfoot's emotions were running the full gamut "How come I didn't know about this?"

"You didn't know because you weren't told. You see there were already question marks about your judgement – particularly concerning this suspect."

"Disgraceful" he snorted "What judgement?"

"Indeed. Three years ago Derek Sanderson was in the frame for a significant currency fraud but before he could be properly interviewed, you intervened and effectively blocked the investigation. With hindsight, that decision looks at best ill-judged and some might see grounds for further investigation."

Proudfoot raised his hands "Fair cop. I did it. It was a ludicrous proposition. How many of your friends have you helped out of a tight spot? Frankly, I fail to see how that is grounds for forcing me out."

"I haven't finished yet. How well do you know Derek Sanderson's wife?"

He shrugged "I have met her a couple of times"

"For such a slight acquaintance you seemed to be particularly glowing about her in support of her residence application. You also seemed to know her pretty well in 2018 when, apparently, you had dinner together at a restaurant in Lewes. Oddly enough at exactly the same time, she was reportedly involved in a road traffic accident in Hove."

Proudfoot went white in the face.

"I don't need to tell you, John, that someone in your position giving a false alibi would almost certainly result in a charge of perverting the course of justice. Now, I am sure you also know that reinvestigating a two-year-old alibi for a minor RTA would be a big ask but in the context of the wider case it might be an option if we felt you were involved rather than just behaving like a complete jerk."

"Preposterous. Ridiculous."

"The thing is John. Is your pension worth the risk that we would find something incriminating?"

He stood without saying a word, picked up his jacket and walked out of the office.

Smallbone watched him go. "I imagine that means no," she said then turned to the two officers. "I repeat, as far as you are concerned anything you heard here is confidential."

They both nodded in unison.

"Now. How are we getting on with Estados?"

"Locally it is a dead end. We are holding Sharon Fellows, Mickey Fisher's girlfriend and Dominic Sharp who worked in the sales operation. There is a chance that we could pull together a conspiracy charge but there is no way of proving intent so if I were the CPS I wouldn't waste court time. Fellows has no previous, nor does Sharp. I recommend they are released without charge."

"Fisher has done a bunk?"

"Yes to Spain apparently to run the Torremolinos office."

"Any sightings by your contacts there?"

"So far no."

"We could charge him in absentia but that is just a pain in the arse – all work and no pay. What about Sanderson?"

"We may be able to tie Reichenbach to some hooky payments but there is no sign of Sanderson's sticky fingers anywhere near that. The best we can do is hand over everything to Fraud so they can add it to their pile of information."

Smallbone grimaced "So we come away with no scalps at all. Nevertheless, I agree with you."

Butler's mobile rang and he answered instinctively. Smallbone waved him to continue.

"Mr Butler it is Jesus Rojo. I said I would let you know if anything happened at our end. The Estados office in Torremolinos was destroyed in an explosion yesterday evening."

A chill ran down Butler's spine "Any casualties?" he asked.

"One male killed. So far unidentified but officers at the scene found a phone that may have been blown into the street. It belonged to a Michael Fisher. No-one of that name is amongst the many injured. The working assumption is that he died in the blast."

"Any idea what caused the explosion?"

"It looks like it was a device set off by a mobile phone call. We are assuming that the victim was lured to the premises before the explosion was triggered."

"An execution?"

"Effectively yes – but these are only assumptions. Is Michael Fisher known to you?"

"Yes. He set up the retail outlet in Brighton that we discussed when we met. Our information is that he had moved to Spain to run the Torremolinos office."

"Alas, that reinforces our suspicions. We will try and track his movements over here and let you know what we find."

"Thank you Judge"

Smallbone and Davies looked at him expectantly.

"It looks like Mickey Fisher has been killed in an explosion at the Estados office in Torremolinos."

Smallbone raised an eyebrow "I sense a but..."

"But they can't identify the body. They are going on the fact that his phone was blown into the street outside and he isn't among the injured."

"I won't believe it until I see that slippery little bastard on a slab in front of me." Davies scoffed "We can probably get hold of his DNA if we act quickly."

"Let's make sure that we know he went to Spain. So far we only have hearsay. Davies can you set your guys on finding the booking and his car – get the registration from Sharon Fellows. We need CCTV the works and send forensics round to Fisher's house. See what we can find."

"I'm on it, " said Davies as he almost ran out of the office.

Smallbone sat down at the desk "What was that about an execution?"

"Judge Rojo's team think that Mickey, if indeed it was Mickey, was lured to the office before the device went off. It was triggered by a phone call."

"So they think it was a professional hit. These really are nasty bastards aren't they."

"If we work on the assumption that it was Mickey. He was the only one on our list who might have been able to finger Derek Sanderson."

251

"What about Rojo's team?"

"They have Juan Mijas in custody as well as Parador the planning guy. Your friend Diamante, their pet judge, topped himself when they got too close. Sanderson acknowledged Mijas as a contact but gave us some old moody about a charity football game.

Parador was at the meeting in the restaurant with Mijas and Sanderson. Rojo thinks he is the weakest link in the chain. They are going to take them to Madrid for interrogation but they are our best chance of bringing Sanderson down."

"Little by little we are getting closer to him" Smallbone fiddled with a pencil absent-mindedly "Now Proudfoot is gone that is one fewer layer of protection."

"My old boss seems to think that Sanderson is protected by some very powerful people, including some in the Government and even MI5"

"I didn't think for a minute that a mere Assistant Chief Constable would be an end to it. If you look at the Reichenbach Fund and how it has risen from the dead, you might be forgiven for thinking that its performance has been beyond belief. Where I come from we think that anything too good to be true generally is."

Endgame

The two black SUVs sat, expectantly, outside the huge gates. Inside, the occupants watched warily as the small door opened and Toro in the black uniform of the National Police Force strolled over to them.

"I have signed the paperwork. Lopez is loading them into the van. Anything happening out here?"

"All quiet so far but I just don't trust the locals to give up without a fight. The sooner we are in Madrid the better." Rio checked her gun for the third time in as many minutes. "We are going to take the Cordoba road. It is very narrow and very confined between here and the motorway. Plenty of opportunities to block our way and spring their man."

Toro nodded, "After last night, best keep our eyes wide open."

They heard the siren a long time before they saw the squad car by which time the four CNP detectives were deployed around the SUVs. Two motorbikes were first to arrive followed by a battered Seat with a flashing blue light. Rio could smell an impending gunfight as she crouched behind the armoured door of the SUV.

An officer in a green uniform climbed slowly out of the Seat making sure that his hands were on display. "We are here to escort you out of the city" he shouted nervously.

Toro didn't have time to check his credentials as, bang on ten o'clock, the prison gate rumbled open and a prisoner transport drove out. "Convoy" he shouted "bikes first, squad car next, SUVs in front and behind the prisoners. Stay watchful".

* * *

The train from Schiphol disgorged its cargo of passengers. Mickey watched from his table in the bar as they spread across the concourse and made their way into the city. He had found himself a room in a small hotel away from the main drag which would do while he addressed the next leg of his journey.

He had always enjoyed Amsterdam. Perhaps he might stay a little longer. As an Irish citizen there were no visa implications and if no-one had noticed his arrival from Lisbon perhaps here was as safe as anywhere.

He should have known that Jasmine was trouble but his mind kept wandering back to the force of the explosion. He did not doubt that it was intended to kill him and that scared him – a lot. If Sanderson had the resources to arrange something like that, what else was he capable of?

Momentarily he considered flying back to London and throwing himself on the mercy of the police but reasoned it would be a really bad idea. It would mean that Sanderson knew where he was whereas here there was a good chance that he didn't.

* * *

Toro barked his orders over the radio. "Make sure we stay on route. No diversions. No short cuts. Through the City, out onto the motorway and away. Take your directions from only me."

"Confirmed." Lopez was on top of things in the prison van.

Rio watched as the motorcyclists cleared a path through the traffic. As good as their word they peeled off as the convoy approached the motorway waving the SUVs and the van past.

"Perhaps some of them have some pride left" said Toro to no-one in particular.

It was one of those days particular to southern Spain with the sun beating down from a cloudless sky creating a heat haze on the road. The motorway climbed away out of the city into the parched landscape of the Sierra Nevada. Relaxing at last, Rio settled down for the four-hour drive to Madrid. The German SUV was powerful and responsive - a joy to drive.

As they moved away from the urban strip along the coast, the traffic thinned. The motorway was largely the preserve of lorries. Any sensible person wanting to travel to the capital would go by train - or fly, both deemed to be too risky for a high-value prisoner like Mijas.

Eagles soared on the thermals as they moved north, circling upwards until they became black specks hanging in the sky. The radio crackled into life from the second SUV.

"Lopez. You are leaking something. It looks like oil."

Toro peered in the rear view mirror. The van was beginning to fall behind. He banged his hand hard on the dashboard "Fuck. I knew they would try something. We are sitting ducks out here. Do not stop. Repeat do not stop"

"The next services are in about twenty kilometres"

"OK. Lopez this what I want you to do...." Toro's voice tailed off as the prison van disintegrated. Almost in slow motion, an explosion ripped the vehicle apart, slamming it into the barrier and turning it over.

Rio executed a dramatic U-turn to face the blazing wreckage and both officers leapt out of the SUV. Toro ran towards the flames while Rio, pistol drawn, scanned the hills for the culprit. One of the black specks moved purposefully away from the scene.

* * *

The incoming message distracted Jasmine momentarily as she worked on the spreadsheet. As it was marked urgent, she clicked on it. Attached to the message was a video. She waited while it was downloaded.

It showed a small convoy of vehicles travelling along a motorway, then a missile striking the van in the middle of the group.

A four-word caption on the film simply said, "Claim paid in full."

She stood beside Sanderson as he replayed it for the third time.

"I always find explosions strangely compelling don't you?"

She nodded. "Exciting"

"Please make sure that all trace of this is removed cleanly from our servers."

"What about Mickey Fisher?"

"I am afraid that you won't be seeing him again. He met with an unfortunate accident."

Jasmine shrugged. "Should we tell his woman?"

"No. Let the police do their job. Leave a decent interval then send her some flowers from the fund. Condolences and so on.

While we are on the subject could you find out when the Mijas funeral is taking place and book me a flight and hotel. I will also need a car- nothing too flashy

I need to attend in person. His wife will be inconsolable."

* * *

Toro beat his hands in frustration on the tarmac. The heat was too intense and it was all too clear that anyone inside the vehicle could not have survived.

"We shouldn't have put him in the van"

"If it wasn't him it would have been one of us." Rio, satisfied that they were not under further attack, was issuing instructions to the rest of the team.

She put her arm around the big man's shoulders. "I have told the guys to back up and block the road while they wait for the Guardia. I think it was a drone by the way. At least, I can't see any sign of life in the hills."

"How did they know which road we would be on? Who told them?" Toro raged.

"If it was a drone they were probably watching us all along. We wouldn't have known."

"Where did they get a drone? Surely, one with that kind of capability has to be military"

Rio shrugged "Not necessarily. They use big machines to carry drugs across from North Africa. It would be fairly easy to adapt them to do this sort of thing."

"If you happen to have a couple of Hellfire missiles lying around."

She shrugged again "Sorry about Lopez. I know you got on well. He was a good guy."

* * *

Baltasar placed the phone back in its cradle and leaned back in his chair. "Fuck" he said quietly.

Rojo looked at him questioningly "What is it?"

"Mijas has been whacked along with Parador. The prison van that they were in was blown up on the motorway south of Cordoba."

"What about our guys?"

"That was Rio on the phone. Lopez was in the van riding shotgun and a prison service guy was driving. They didn't have a chance. Toro is pretty beaten up about it but everyone else is OK."

"Do we know how it happened? Was it a bomb? An IED?"

"Rio thinks it was a missile fired from a drone."

"Mother of God. If I find the slightest hint that the locals were involved in this I will bring the roof down on them. You had better let them know that."

Baltasar nodded "You realise that this means that we were nowhere near the top. Mijas was just being used by someone bigger. I should have known what we were dealing with when they blew up the office. All that work was in vain."

Rojo was standing looking out of the window. "No, not in vain, it was just the starter before the main course. This has to be the money talking. The money men didn't want Mijas or Parador cutting any kind of deal with us that would compromise them so they were eliminated. Let's see what our English friends have to say about it. Today we start again."

* * *

Butler put down the phone and slumped back in his chair. Davies was concerned.

"What just happened? You are looking like you just lost a relative."

"We just lost our links to Reichenbach. Two of the Spanish guys that Sanderson met were blown up in a police van on their way to Madrid."

"Didn't one of them top himself?"

"Yes. That was the third person at the table"

"Wow. Sanderson was a bad choice of a dinner guest."

"Indeed he was"

"So that means we are up shit creek. We have absolutely nothing on Reichenbach or Sanderson. We have a kid who looks about twelve insisting that he had no idea about any criminality. We have Mickey's girlfriend singing like a canary about the scam but keeping quiet about the funding and Mickey himself has been blown to bits. Is that about it?"

Butler nodded. "They haven't formally identified Mickey's body yet but they think he may have triggered the explosion himself."

"Mickey? That bloke is slipperier than a ton of eels. How did he trigger the explosion?"

"They found fragments of a device that was triggered by a mobile call that came from his phone."

"Christ. We are dealing with some nasty bastards here. If I were you I would check under my car before I used it. I know I will."

Butler smiled grimly "It was always going to be a long game, going after a bent fund like Reichenbach. This was just round

259

one. So although the results may not be there in terms of arrests we know a lot more about them and how they operate than we did before. One day we will find a link that will nail them."

Davies snorted. "Let's hope we are both alive to see it"

"Amen to that"

A moment of peace

He parked where he had parked before and walked down the valley. He had driven past the clearing with the temporary building put up in haste to house the developers' equipment. It looked tired and dusty.

The sign describing Aguilera as a prime development of villas had been torn down and lay in the dust. The whole scene had a gritty charm and he captured it in a few shots.

Rojo was in the middle of a series of funerals. Baltasar had insisted on accompanying him. "When else do I get the chance to prove that my dress uniform still fits me" he had insisted.

The day before they had to negotiate the throngs of locals attending the interment of Mijas. The funeral was a reminder of how popular the mayor had been locally. Out of respect, they had suspended the case temporarily.

At the church, Baltasar had nudged him in the ribs and pointed across to where the family were showing their respects. He recognised the tall, balding man with spectacles – Derek Sanderson. He had never felt so impotent.

"We have nothing" hissed Baltasar "and he knows it."

This morning he had come from the funeral of Parador. This had been far more emotional. Parador's wife was distraught as were his children clinging together in misery. Rojo found himself wishing that he hadn't seen the photographs of Parador with another man. He felt guilty that he hadn't made sure that he had been sent to Madrid as soon as he had been arrested.

"There was no guarantee that he would have been any safer there," said Baltasar.

Lopez was next, but for that they had to return to Madrid and this stopover was a diversion on the drive. Baltasar had taken the opportunity to visit his son in Alicante on the way back. Rio and Toro would be meeting them at the church.

He couldn't care less if he never saw Malaga again but the sierras were just starting to turn autumnal and he loved the changing colours.

He thought about the lynx – at least it would have some peace now that the chance of the land being developed had passed.

He stood and drank in the silence. Very soon the team would reassemble and begin looking at the chain of events that lead to the deaths and sometime later there would be a reckoning.

Of that he was sure.

www.ingramcontent.com/pod-product-compliance
Lightning Source LLC
Chambersburg PA
CBHW061953170626
46813CB00006B/2632